I0601034

aunt enid
protector
extraordinaire

aunt enid
protector
extraordinaire

KAREN J CARLISLE

Kraken Publishing

aunt enid: protector extraordinaire
An Aunt Enid Mystery,

Copyright © 2018 Karen J Carlisle

The moral right of this author has been asserted.

All rights reserved in all media. No part of this book may be reproduced, stored or transmitted in any form, or by any means, without written permission (except under the statutory exceptions of the Australian Copyright Act 1968).

This is a work of fiction. All characters and events in this publication, other than those clearly in public domain, are fictitious. Any resemblance to real persons, living or dead is purely coincidental.

Cover design and artwork, icons and internal artwork:
Copyright © 2017 by Karen J Carlisle

A catalogue record for this book is available from the National Library of Australia

ISBN: 978-0-9944850-3-8
Series: Carlisle, Karen J. The Aunt Enid Mysteries Book 1

Also available separately as eBook

This book is written in British English.
Printed in Australia.
Typeset in Times Roman 12pt.

Published by Kraken Publishing.
www.krakenpublishing.com

For my Great Aunt Enid and Grandma Pearl
Thank you for wonderful memories,
lashings of lemon butter
and other mouthwatering recipes

contents

aunt enid
protector extraordinaire

bonus extras

chapter one

Patches of sunlight skittered across the page of Sally's book. A faint tink rattled in her glass as she picked up the iced tea from the table beside her. She peered into the liquid and frowned; only a speck of ice remained. She took a long sip. The ice melted on her tongue, spreading the coolness down her throat and through her chest.

Three days of stifling north winds had heated up the old sandstone cottage, even in the cooler air of the Adelaide Hills. She had no choice but to decamp to the swing chair under her Great Aunt's ancient lemon tree, and shelter in the shade. If only Aunt Enid had decided to go on holiday in Queensland in the winter, and not late spring. Sally made a mental note to ensure the air conditioner was fixed before she volunteered to house sit again.

Her toes stung, their skin glowed bright pink in the glaring summer sun. Sally lifted her feet off the warm grass, tucked them onto the edge of the swing seat, then leaned back into the shade of the tree and nestled into the mound of soft cushions.

She glanced at the rows of garden gnomes crowding the front yard. The closest group was clustered near a patch of crazy paving, just beyond the shade of the lemon tree. They stared back with unblinking eyes. They always seemed to be watching and waiting - as if they knew something she didn't.

Sally scoffed. They were only bits of ceramic pottery and paint. She shifted in the seat and turned the page, trying to ignore them.

A cool southerly breeze caressed her bare arms, evaporating the thin layer of sweat covering her skin. The wind had finally changed direction.

Birds twittered in the branches sprawling above her. The faint squawk of chickens drifted across from the neighbouring property. A lawn mower droned in the distance; the sweet smell of grass, and cow manure, wafted past with each flurry of air.

An errant strand of hair tickled Sally's nose. She turned the page and struggled to focus on the words. Her eyelids were heavy. She breathed in the cool air and closed her eyes, allowing the sounds and smells to melt into each other.

Shadows flickered across Sally's closed eyelids. Heat swirled around her, bringing a heady scent of eucalyptus from the surrounding bushland, and a faint whiff of possum urine. The seat squeaked and lurched under her body. She flinched. Her book flopped to the ground.

A raucous cawing clawed at the edges of Sally's consciousness. Something cracked below the swing seat. Sally's foot slipped off the seat and slammed onto the ground, jarring her shinbone. Her eyes snapped open.

Pinpoints of pain pricked Sally's toes. She raised her foot and examined her big toe. Beads of blood lined a small cut. She picked out a piece of red ceramic and squeezed her toe as she searched the grass. One of Aunt Enid's precious garden gnomes lay shattered on the ground. Pieces of shiny red cap lay strewn in the grass surrounding her foot.

Sally's heart sank. Aunt Enid would be devastated; she loved her garden gnomes.

"How on earth did that get there?" Sally rubbed her injured toe. A cracked ceramic gnome head lay on a piece of crazy paving, staring up at her with flat black eyes.

She shifted slowly in the seat and eyed the group of garden gnomes huddled nearby. They'd always given her the creeps. She frowned; she hadn't realised they were so close.

A raven hopped out from under the swing seat. Sally jerked her dangling leg back onto the seat. The bird pecked at the hat shards and cawed.

Sally examined the broken garden gnome. The raven nudged the fragments and waited. Sally edged further back into the cushions, away from the edge of the seat. What did it want?

The raven nudged the pieces again, stepped aside and cocked its head.

Sally slowly lowered one foot, not removing her gaze from the bird, and probed for the ground with her toe. Grass tickled her toes. The raven didn't flinch.

She lowered the other foot onto a clear section of grass, slowly picked up the largest fragment of ceramic and turned it over in her fingers. Its broken lips half-smiled back at her. A shiver ran up her fingers.

The raven cawed; its white eyes followed her every move.

Sally chewed her lips. Perhaps she could fix the ornament before Aunt Enid came home? She checked the time on her mobile phone. There were still a few hours before her aunt's flight was due.

She collected up the pieces and wrapped them in the hem of her skirt.

The raven turned its head toward Sally and blinked.

A burst of hot wind tugged at Sally's skirt and fidgeted with the pages of the book lying on the ground by her feet. The acrid scent of possum caught at the back of her throat. Hair whipped across her face.

The raven twitched its glistening black wings. It growled, launched into the air and soared off over the lemon tree.

The north wind buffeted Sally, pushing her back toward the lemon tree. She clasped the loose material of her skirt, tucked it in close and picked her way through the rows of garden gnomes toward the house, careful not to knock another one over onto the concrete paving. Surely, Great Aunt Enid would have something to reattach the broken pieces?

She braced herself as another gust of hot wind pummelled her chest. The wind rushed towards the gully. The gate slammed behind her. Her skirt fell limp around her legs.

Wheels squeaked rhythmically along the path.

"Ah, it's good to be home." The voice was soft and lilting. "I missed you, Winky. You, too, Sebastian."

Sally knew that voice; she clutched the broken gnome in her skirt and slowly turned.

Aunt Enid ambled along the path, holding her shiny metal walking stick in one hand and dragging a wheeled suitcase in the other. She bent down to greet another garden gnome. Her grey bob skimmed her jawline.

"Now, Blue, what are you doing all the way over here?" She lifted her head and peered over the line of garden ornaments. "And where's Red?" Her eyebrow wrinkled as her gaze fell on Sally.

"Aunt Enid, you're early," said Sally, trying not to bring attention to her bundle.

"I caught an earlier flight, when I saw the weather report." Aunt Enid huffed. "It isn't supposed to get this hot."

Sally wiped the sweat from her forehead. The cool change had been very short-lived.

"I trust Mr B has behaved himself?"

Sally nodded.

Aunt Enid's gaze hovered over the bundled skirt.

Sally swallowed and shifted her weight. The gnome bits clinked inside her skirt bundle.

Aunt Enid released her grip on the suitcase. The handle telescoped back into the suitcase with a thunk. "Is everything all right, Sally?"

Poor Aunt Enid, living by herself in the old cottage. Sally's heart sank. All alone, with only her cat, her hydrangeas and her garden ornaments to keep her company.

Aunt Enid rested both her hands on her silver cane.

"Let's have a look," she said. "It can't be all that bad."

Sally slowly unfolded the hem of her skirt. The gnome's crooked face stared out at her, surrounded by pieces of red ceramic.

"Oh, dear." Aunt Enid took a deep breath. "Poor Red."

Sally held her breath.

Aunt Enid glanced out of the corner of her eye in the direction of the swing seat - and Sally's abandoned book.

"What were you doing all the way over there?" she whispered.

"The air conditioning broke down and it was cooler outside in the shade with the southerly wind," replied Sally.

"He always was a curious one." Aunt Enid sighed. "We'll fix you up straight away. I've got some super glue in the kitchen."

Sally raised an eyebrow; her aunt was talking to the garden ornaments again.

Aunt Enid's cat padded up to her and rubbed itself against her ankle. A relaxed smile flitted over her aunt's lips. She bent down, ran her hand along the cat's charcoal fur, and tweaked the tip of its tail.

"I'm glad to be home too, Mr B. Did you miss me?"

Mr B entwined himself around Aunt Enid's legs and purred.

"I love you, too," she whispered. "But there's no time to dally. Red is in need of assistance." Aunt Enid snatched up the suitcase handle and strode toward the house. Mr B trotted along behind her.

Sally frowned and re-wrapped the broken gnome. Talking to the cat was one thing, but inanimate garden ornaments...? Perhaps Aunt Enid had been alone too long? Sally hesitated. Uncle Edward had gone a little funny, just before he was diagnosed with dementia.

Sally's heart cracked. Was Aunt Enid creeping down the same path? Sally drew in a sharp breath. Surely not? Not Aunt Enid; she was too feisty to give in.

Sally gripped the bundle in her skirt and traipsed along the path after her aunt. The sun glared off the cottage's corrugated iron roof. Two gigantic hydrangea bushes framed the entrance to the veranda surrounding the sandstone cottage. Red brick quoins edged the building and surrounded the door and windows. Aunt Enid was proud of her home - one of the earliest built in the area. She said it tied her to history, to her roots.

Aunt Enid glanced at the pinkish flowers as she approached the veranda, and froze.

"That's not good." She sucked air in through her teeth. "Have you been adding the coffee grounds to the garden?"

Mr B twitched and skittered off into the house, the cat flap swinging in his wake.

Sally examined the hydrangea bush. The flowers had faded to a delicate shade of pink - quite common in Adelaide's alkaline soil - rimmed with only a hint of blue. Aunt Enid preferred blue flowers. But it wasn't the end of the world, surely?

"Sorry, Aunt Enid. I forgot. I got some locum work. And I don't drink coffee, remember? It keeps me awake."

Aunt Enid scanned the sky. "It shouldn't be so hot this time of year," she replied. "I thought it would be safe." She tugged her cotton gloves on tight. "Bring my suitcase, Sally. I'll pop the kettle on. We've got work to do." Aunt Enid eyed the hydrangeas, glanced back at the sky and clicked her tongue. "I just hope I'm not too late," she mumbled as she marched into the cottage.

The screen door rattled behind her.

Sally peered up into the sky. Storm clouds were gathering in the north. She raised an eyebrow; usually the thunderstorms rolled up from the south. She wrapped her fingers around the suitcase's handle and followed her aunt into the cottage.

Water gurgled in the coffee maker. Coffee dripped into the glass jug and filled the kitchen with its aroma. It was one of the few mod cons in the post-war kitchen to which Aunt Enid had succumbed - quite logical, as it negated the necessity to fire up the old, enamelled wood-burning stove in the scorching Adelaide summer heat.

Sally straightened the corner of the newspaper on the kitchen table and placed the last piece of broken ceramic on the paper. Each piece was precisely arranged, according to its colour and original location on the garden gnome - like components organised by a technician in readiness to re-build a machine.

Saucers clinked on the mottled-green laminate tabletop. Teacups rattled as Aunt Enid set the remainder of the rose-decorated, cream-coloured china. Her gaze skimmed over the newspaper.

Sally's shoulders tensed, waiting for a reprimand for the destroyed garden gnome or a snide comment about the younger generation's lack of responsibility. But there were no recriminations. Aunt Enid remained silent. She turned back to the bench and flipped on the kettle.

Sally relaxed her shoulders; Aunt Enid seemed to be taking the demise of her beloved 'Red' quite well.

Shadows danced across the sink as the lace curtains flicked in Aunt Enid's direction, fanned by a welcome cool breeze now dispersing the stifling heat accumulated over the past few days.

The bead curtain clinked and tinkled in the kitchen doorway, as its belled-tips brushed over the sleek body of Aunt Enid's cat. He strolled across the linoleum floor, paused near the old stove and raised his head in Sally's direction. He blinked.

Sally smiled. After a month of house sitting, she recognised the high praise of feline acknowledgement.

Green doors thunked softly as he rubbed his body along the cream bench cupboards and leapt onto the green laminate bench top near Aunt Enid.

"You know better than that, Mr B." She elbowed him away as she carved a few slices of bread. "Off the bench *now*."

Mr B flicked his tail, thrust his nose in the air and stepped off the edge of the bench. His paws landed silently on the lino. He slinked over to the kitchen table and vaulted onto Sally's lap.

Claws pricked her lap as he pawed at her skirt and nudged her hand. Sally glanced down at the cat. A remnant of ceramic lay on her skirt. She picked it out of the folds and placed it on the table next to its partner, painted with the other half of its fractured smile.

The cat circled twice, plopped into her lap and purred. His vibrations permeated her skin, calming her nerves. Sally wiggled her fingers into his soft fur and scratched his chin. He purred louder and closed his eyes.

Aunt Enid removed a couple of small plates from the cupboard above the bench and raised an eyebrow. "I see you've made yourself comfortable, Mr B."

Sally's jaw clenched as the plates clattered on the kitchen table. The cat's tail twitched. She felt his muscles tense, as Aunt Enid glanced at the cat curled up in her lap. A wrinkle flickered over her aunt's forehead and then was gone.

The kettle hissed. Aunt Enid jerked to attention and turned back to face the bench. She swirled the teapot and poured the warming water down the sink, then added the tealeaves and poured in the steaming water. A lilac and rose-coloured crocheted tea cosy completed the ritual.

"Fetch me the lemon butter, please, Sally," said Aunt Enid as she stared out the window.

Cool air enveloped Sally as she stepped into the compact pantry. A cord brushed her ear; its weighted end nudged her cheek. Sally tugged it. The light clicked on.

The niche was barely one metre square, not counting the shelves overflowing with sparkling bottles, cans and Tupperware containers. Several shelves were dedicated to stacked rows of glass pots of home-grown honey and jars of lemon butter, their decorative labels written in Aunt Enid's precise hand. Each brimmed with bright yellow contents, which glowed in the incandescent light.

Sally chose a jar from the top shelf, and placed it on the kitchen table next to a plate of freshly sliced bread and a covered, earthenware butter dish.

Aunt Enid sat on the opposite side of the table, drinking from one of the fine china teacups. The cat had settled in her lap and was licking his paws. The aroma of freshly brewed coffee wafted over the table.

Aunt Enid pulled the honey dipper out of the pot and let the sweet liquid dribble into her coffee.

Sally smiled. She'd only ever seen Aunt Enid drink from a teacup. Come to think of it, there were no mugs anywhere in Aunt Enid's cupboards.

"Why do you always drink coffee from a teacup?" Sally asked.

"They were a gift," she replied, "from a dear friend." She rubbed the cat's belly.

The tea strainer lightly tinked on the edge of Sally's cup. Aunt Enid poured Sally's cup of tea and offered her the honey pot. Sally shook her head; she'd not acquired the taste for honey. She preferred sugar to sweeten her tea.

Sally dipped the butter knife into the lemon butter, slathered it on a piece of bread and took a bite. The tang almost brought tears to her eyes. She licked her lips and observed her aunt as she took another bite.

Aunt Enid was quiet - not her usual self at all. She usually revelled in afternoon tea. It was a chance to catch up, to regale her companions with stories from her youth and one of the few occasions when she approved of gossip. Today there was no chronicling of holiday anecdotes. Her eyelids looked heavy, her shoulders slumped, as she nibbled on the corner of her scantily condimented bread.

Sally frowned. Was it the hydrangeas? The broken garden ornament or...? Her heart sank; had something happened during her aunt's stay in Queensland?

Sally opened her mouth to speak. No words came.

Aunt Enid stared at the broken ceramic pieces on the newspaper and patted Mr B absentmindedly.

Sally bit her lip. Poor Aunt Enid. Sally's heart ached. She had to know what was wrong.

"I do hope your friend in Queensland is feeling better." she said.

Aunt Enid drew a deep breath, placed the bread back on her plate and whispered in reply: "She died."

Sally coughed as a breadcrumb trickled down her windpipe. "I... I'm sorry, Aunt Enid. I... I didn't..."

Aunt Enid returned to patting the cat on her lap. Its soothing purr filled the room.

"A weak heart, they said." Aunt Enid pinched bits off the bread crust and crumbled them in her fingers. "Not to worry, dear. She had a good innings. She'd been in the job longer than me and—"

Aunt Enid took a swig of coffee and rose from her chair.

The cat yowled as he tumbled to the floor.

"Now, where's that super glue?" Metal rattled as Aunt Enid yanked open one drawer after another.

Sally shifted in her seat. She'd never seen her aunt so rattled before. Aunt Enid snatched up a tube from the bottom drawer, sat back down and scraped her chair closer to the table.

The cat slowly circled the perimeter of the kitchen.

"Shall we start at the head and work our way down?" asked Aunt Enid with a glint in her eye.

Sally picked up one of the ceramic pieces - an arm clad in green. A well-worn scythe fell from its cracked fist. She squeezed a thin line of glue along the exposed rim and set it into the gaping hole at the gnome's shoulder.

The cat mewed, paused to cock his head in the direction of unheard noises.

Aunt Enid peered out the kitchen window. The curtains hung limp. Sally followed her aunt's gaze, tracking the cat as it stalked up to the beaded curtain in the doorway, and sniffed at a red smudge on the floor tiles.

Sally frowned as she traced the line of smeared red spots back towards her chair.

Aunt Enid peered under the table. Her eyes widened. "Sally, your foot is bleeding."

Sally glanced at her foot. Blood had crusted on her big toe. "It's alright," she said. "It's stopped."

Aunt Enid shook her head. "There's a bandaid in the bathroom cabinet." The line of her lips hardened. "I insist. You don't want it to get infected."

Sally nodded. She'd never hear the end of it if she disagreed. She shoved the last piece of bread into her mouth and let the taste engulf her taste buds - sweet, with an unexpected tang - just like Aunt Enid. She loved the incongruity, just as she loved her great aunt.

Great Aunt Enid's bathroom was immaculate, if a little outdated, with sparkling cream tiles and apricot ceramics. A crocheted toilet roll dolly stared at Sally from the windowsill, with big blue eyes.

Sally opened the bathroom wall cabinet. Sunlight flashed off the mirror hidden on the inside of the cabinet door.

It had been like that as long as she remembered. Inside out. Aunt Enid didn't seem to mind. Perhaps she was too polite to ever insist on it being re-installed correctly. No matter; it had been that way since Sally was a toddler, not even able to reach the enamelled taps.

Sally sighed and searched through the cabinet's contents until she found a small bottle of tea tree oil, a zip-lock bag of cotton tips and a box of adhesive bandages.

The cabinet door clicked shut. Sally perched on the edge of the bathtub and examined the gash on her big toe. Fortunately, broken ceramic was sharp edged, resulting in a clean cut. She winced as the tea tree oil worked its way deep into the cut, then dressed it with a clean bandaid. She placed her foot tentatively on the cool floor tiles. Her toe throbbed. Perhaps she should put some shoes on before she finished packing her bags.

The half-filled suitcase sat on the bed, the bedspread bunched up behind it. A tidy pile of folded t-shirts was neatly stacked to one side. Sally turned toward the cupboard to collect the remaining items of clothing and halted.

The standing mirror stood ghost-like near the window, its ornately carved dark wood concealed by a white sheet. The thin cotton twitched in the breeze.

"How...?" Sally's forehead wrinkled. When had Aunt Enid found the time to start packing away the spare room?

Sally ran her fingers over the edge of the covered mirror, feeling the concealed bumps and crevices of the carved foliage underneath.

"Why...?" Why did her aunt seem so keen for her to leave? She hadn't said anything. Sally flopped onto the edge of the bed. Was that why Aunt Enid was so quiet at afternoon tea? Was her aunt trying to work out how to get her to leave?

Sally scanned the room. Everything else *seemed* to be untouched. She slowly shook her head. It was all quite peculiar. But, then again, Aunt Enid had always been peculiar; well, perhaps just a little eccentric?

But that was why she loved her. Everyone else in the family was so... unimaginative.

Sally grinned at the image of the septuagenarian breathing in glue fumes as she wrestled a miniature scythe back into the fist of a ceramic garden gnome. She was reminded of Uncle Edward and his wonderful stories, before he... Sally bit her lip. Niggling questions bobbed to the surface of her mind.

She packed her remaining belongings, zipped shut the suitcase and tried to ignore years of training and experience as a nurse.

She slipped on her sand shoes, pushed the memories of Uncle Edward from her mind and tried not to worry about the state of her aunt's mental health. No doubt there would be a reason for today's events.

She took a deep breath and sighed.

There had to be.

chapter two

"**b**ingo!"

The plastic chair scraped on the floorboards as Enid jumped to her feet and squeaked with delight. The crowd murmured. Claps echoed in the hall.

"Congratulations to Enid Turner. Again." The microphone screeched. "Please hand your card to Mr Knowles for verification."

Enid sat back in her chair, turned to her friend and grinned. The woman's pale red curls wiggled as she shook her head. She fidgeted with the string of pearls around her neck; she was ten years Enid's junior but you'd never guess by the way she dressed.

"What is it, Agnes?" asked Enid.

"Enid, you didn't..?" Agnes sighed.

Enid's eyes widened in mock innocence. "I'd never do such a thing."

"Oh, Enid." Agnes smiled; the laugh lines around her eyes deepened. "You never were one for rules."

"And that's why you like me best out of all the—"

A soft hand fell on Enid's shoulder. "Congratulations, Miss Turner." The voice was as soft as his touch.

Enid turned to greet the newcomer. His pale blue eyes smiled at her.

"There you go, Mr Knowles." She handed him her bingo card. "I assure it's all in order."

"So there's only two of the Musketeers here tonight?" he asked.

"Pardon?" snipped Enid.

Mr Knowles cleared his throat. "Sorry, I noticed your friend, Mrs Oldham, did not attend tonight."

"No." Olive Oldham was the oldest of the trio of friends. And she was *never* late.

Enid scanned the hall again. Olive was still nowhere in sight. Enid gritted her teeth. "She was my lift home."

Mr Knowles glanced over the card, held it into the air and nodded.

"Ah, yes," replied the squat man behind the microphone. "You know where to collect your winnings, Miss Turner."

Chairs screeched throughout the hall as the senior citizens rose and made their way en masse to the refreshments table on the far side of the hall. Voices overlapped and fused into a general drone.

Mr Knowles hovered behind Enid's chair and cleared his throat. Agnes nudged Enid's arm.

"Would you like a cup of tea?" he asked.

"Thank you for the kind offer, Mr Knowles." Enid straightened her pen. "But I—"

"She prefers coffee. Black. Two sugars," Agnes said quickly.

"Coffee, it is then. I'll meet you by the refreshment table." Mr Knowles dodged clumps of pensioners in a beeline for the table.

"You know Mr Knowles is sweet on you." Agnes slapped Enid's wrist. "Don't tease him."

Enid rummaged in her handbag for... nothing in particular. Perhaps Agnes would give up on this latest mission of hers?

Agnes huffed. "It's been years since Owen disappeared."

Enid twisted the signet ring on her finger.

"You still wear his ring, Enid?" Agnes placed her hand on Enid's. "You can't live with his memory forever."

She eyed Mr Knowles and gasped. "Perhaps he could help restore your hydrangeas?"

"Who, dear?"

Agnes motioned her head in the direction of the refreshment table. Enid followed her friend's gaze; Mr Knowles stood near the table with a steaming cup of coffee in one hand, and waved back at her. He seemed sweet, but he wasn't Owen.

She avoided her friend's expectant gaze. "No, thank you," she whispered.

"Well, at least be polite. One cup of coffee isn't the end of the world."

Enid swallowed. Her throat was parched. "Only if you - what is it they say - run interference." Enid rose from her chair, straightened her skirts and trudged toward her inevitable fate.

Mr Knowles grinned and presented Enid with a small plate of baked goods: an Anzac biscuit, a fluffy scone with lemon butter and a slice of chocolate cake with shiny icing.

"Hmmm, try the scones. They're delicious," he said.

Enid accepted the coffee and took a long sip to avoid replying.

Agnes laughed and picked up the scone. "Enid made the scones," she said, "and the lemon butter."

Mr Knowles' eyes widened. "Really?" He picked up another lemon-butter-laden scone and took a bite.

"Yes, she's famous for them."

Mr Knowles licked his lips. "Delicious, Miss Turner."

"It's an old family recipe," said Agnes.

"Handed down since 1838..." continued Enid as she peered out the hall windows. Shadows flitted across the glass. The wind was picking up again.

"That's precise," replied Mr Knowles between mouthfuls.

"She still has the original recipe book. Her—"

Enid nudged her friend in the rib; she was rambling again. Mr Knowles paused mid-munch.

Agnes coughed. "— dated everything."

Enid frowned at Agnes. "We really should be going, Mr Knowles. Thank you for the coffee."

Mr Knowles gulped down the last morsel of scone and raised an eyebrow.

"You live in the Hills don't you, Miss Turner?"

"Yes," replied Enid, examining the windows.

"I understand you lost your lift home. I would be honoured to drive you." Mr Knowles dipped his head in a bow.

Enid eyed Agnes through narrowed her eyelids. She had no doubt her friend was matchmaking again. "Thank you, Mr Knowles, but my grandniece is driving me home."

He glanced at Agnes. "Then I'll take my leave. It was a pleasure to meet you, Miss Turner."

"And you, Mr Knowles," said Agnes.

They watched him weave his way through the chattering gathering.

"It's obvious he likes you, Enid," whispered Agnes.

Enid scoffed. "You really should stop trying to match make, Agnes."

"A cat doesn't count as compan—"

Enid thrust out her hand. "Give me your mobile phone, I have to ring Sally to pick me up."

"But you said—"

Enid smirked. "I obfuscated. Isn't that part of our job?"

Enid's heels clicked on the concrete step as she emerged from the hall. The wheels of Agnes' canvas shopping trolley thunked down the steps, ahead of her. Agnes stopped and whispered to Mr Knowles on the bottom step.

Enid pursed her lips, grasped the railing with her free hand to balance herself and tentatively prodded each step with her walking stick as she descended each of them, one at time.

"Go on," said Agnes as Enid passed them. "She won't bite."

Enid pulled her white gloves tight. Her grey bob fell forward, concealing her annoyance. "Sometimes I do," she whispered under her breath, as she crossed the bitumen to the verge. She didn't have time for such frivolity. There were more important concerns than fending off amorous pensioners - and Agnes knew it.

Mr Knowles' eyes sparkled in the flickering street light. He raised his finger to his forehead, as if tipping his hat in Enid's direction. Enid gripped her walking stick, counted to ten and poked at a crack in the bitumen. Its heat seeped through the soles of her shoes. Warm air clung to Enid's skin, unable to escape in the sudden stillness.

Mr Knowles smiled as he ascended the steps and waited in the doorway.

"Goodnight, Mr Knowles." Agnes strode toward Enid, her shopping trolley wheels squeaking furiously.

"Why did you ignore him, Enid?" Agnes huffed. "He likes you." She reached into her shopping bag and pulled out a large blue plastic container wrapped in a clear plastic bag.

"For your hydrangeas. We can't have them failing us, can we?" Agnes handed her the ice-cream container. It reeked of stale coffee and chicken manure.

"But what about your hydrangeas?" asked Enid.

Agnes shook her head. "I insist. Your need is greater than mine." She patted Enid on the hand. "And I can recommend a good gardener. He's done wonders with Olive's hydrangeas, in only a few weeks." She clicked her tongue. "He's her grandson, Simon, so I'd say he's trustworthy."

Mr Knowles waved at them. Agnes nudged Enid and waggled her fingers in his direction.

Enid rolled her eyes. Agnes was not going to give up. She raised her hand momentarily in his direction and turned back to face Agnes. That was enough encouragement for one day.

A pale blue hatchback trundled down the street and shuddered to a stop in front of the hall. The car door swung open.

"Here's my ride." *And not too soon.* Enid hugged Agnes and slipped into the passenger seat beside her great niece.

Sally leaned past Enid, glanced through the window and grinned.

"Is that your boyfriend?" she asked.

Enid shook her head. Boyfriend indeed! Where would she find the time? "He's a friend of Agnes."

"Oh." Sally slumped back into her seat.

"Mr B wouldn't condone it."

Sally laughed. "Careful, Aunt Enid, you could be in danger of becoming a crazy cat lady."

Agnes ducked down level to the window. "See you tomorrow," she mouthed through the closed window.

Enid waved goodbye.

"How was your evening with the girls?" asked Sally.

Enid frowned. "Olive didn't come tonight."

The gearbox grumbled as Sally thumped the gear stick into position. Enid winced.

"I hope she isn't sick," said Sally after a long pause.

So did Enid. She'd already lost one friend this month... She stared through the windscreen. Spots of rain plopped onto the glass and trickled down the windscreen, like tears. It wasn't like Olive to not phone.

"I'm sure she's fine," said Sally in a soothing voice. "Perhaps she just forgot. It does happen, you know."

The gearbox strained as the car slowed to a stop. The right indicator clicked loudly, repeating her friend's name: *Ol-ive. Ol-ive. Ol-ive.*

Enid peered through the dribbling curtain in the direction of Olive's house. Why hadn't she phoned? She never missed Bingo night. She clutched the ice cream dish.

"Do you mind if we check on her?"

Sally tapped the dashboard clock. "We should have time and still get you home before you turn into a pumpkin." She wrestled the car into first gear. "Though it looks like you left your prince charming waiting on the steps."

Enid glared at Sally and cleared her throat. "I won't complain about the transport, and you won't mention the word *boyfriend* again. Deal?"

Sally nodded and flicked the indicator in the other direction.

A hot flash enveloped Enid. She wound down the window. A blast of hot air rushed over her face.

Sally pressed a button on the dash. The air conditioning clicked into life. Cool air wafted over Enid's ankles.

The radio crackled. Sally wiggled a knob on the dash. It flickered into life. A woman laughed and chatted:

"Though I'd dial up the air con at the end of the week. The weather bureau is warning us of another heatwave, worse than the last—"

Sally frowned and clicked off the radio.

"You need to get your air con fixed at home," she said.

"No need, dear," said Enid. "I'll be fine." She stared out of the window

Sally eyed Enid. "Then you'll stay at my house for the duration. I won't let you stay in that oven without it."

"It's fixed."

Sally raised an eyebrow.

"It was just a loose fuse," said Enid.

The car rattled to a halt in front of Olive's cottage. Its engine sputtered, gasped and fell silent. Enid peered through the water-smeared

passenger window, frowned and wound the window all the way down.

The house was dark. The curtains were drawn. Not a sliver of light seeped past them.

Enid cocked her head to listen. The trees were still. The front gate hung precariously from the top hinge, half-open and unmoving, its grey shadow wavered on the footpath in the flickering glow of the street light. A dark ute and a trailer was parked across the street under the faltering street light. There was no sound - nothing but the occasional drip of rain on the windscreen.

It was too quiet.

Sally's voice broke the silence: "Perhaps she's already gone to bed?"

Enid shook her head and straightened her cotton gloves "We don't need much sleep at our age, dear. Besides Olive wouldn't pass up a chance for a flutter. She's never too ill for a game of online poker, and she says the good ones don't start 'til late."

Enid scanned the windows for any hint of activity. A dim shadow flitted across the front window. Her eyes narrowed. The curtain twitched. She gripped the head of her silver walking stick.

"I think I'll just pop inside and check on her," she said.

"I'm coming with you," said Sally.

The car door clicked and squeaked open. Enid slid out of the seat. The dangling gate creaked as it swung open. She trudged up the path and paused to examine the two massive hydrangea bushes on either side of the front step.

They looked as if they hadn't been watered in a month; the leaves formed a wilted blanket, falling away from dead brown-tipped flower heads. Pale petals lay strewn over the ground at their feet.

"Hmmm..." Enid rubbed a limp leaf in her fingers. Perhaps Agnes had been mistaken about the skills of Olive's new gardener? She raised an eyebrow. Yet the rest of the garden looked healthy. It was as if these bushes had been singled out... Enid's pulse raced.

Enid stepped up onto the porch. Garden gnomes guarded its perimeter. She eyed them and strained to listen. Still no sound but the patter of Sally's sandshoes on the wet path. She sniffed the air. There was something... slightly...

Sally stepped onto the porch next to Enid and raised her hand to knock on the door. Enid placed her gloved hand on Sally's wrist.

"Wait," whispered Enid.

"But, I thought...?"

"Something's not right." Enid wrapped her gloved fingers around the door handle and breathed quietly: *Aperire*. The door clicked.

Sally raised an eyebrow.

"It wasn't locked," replied Enid.

Sally peered into the darkness. "Maybe we should call the police?" she whispered.

Enid shook her head. "Not until we need them." She looked Sally in the eye. "They'll assume I'm dotty. Best we get the lie of the land first."

Enid pushed the door open and sniffed. A faint odour tainted the air. A hint of something... acrid? Enid clutched her walking stick and stepped over the threshold into the darkness. She heard Sally hesitate, then follow her.

The smell was stronger inside the hallway. Enid screwed up her nose and followed the smell.

There was a click and light flared around her. She thrust a gloved hand over her eyes and cursed under her breath.

"Sally!"

"Sorry, Aunt Enid." Sally stood behind her brandishing an umbrella.

"Shhh." Enid's gaze flashed down the hallway and skimmed across the lounge room next to them. All *seemed* in order. She let out a slow, controlled breath.

Sally raised the umbrella. "Did you hear that?" she whispered.

Enid shook her head.

"There it is again." Sally's warm breath brushed Enid's ear.

A faint tinkle, like a fairy bell. Someone was in the kitchen.

"Does your friend have a cat?" asked Sally.

"No."

Sally froze.

Enid's walking stick thumped softly on the carpet as she crept down the hallway and stopped a few feet from the kitchen door. A curtain of faceted, translucent beads shimmered in the hallway light, its ends quivered as if in an unfelt breeze. A pungent aroma drifted into the hall.

Enid's heart jumped. She raised her stick to strike.

"I can't find your friend," Sally whispered into Enid's ear.

Enid lowered her walking stick and swallowed, trying to will her heart back down her throat.

Sally leaned closer. "And there's no one in the rest of the house."

"It's not wise to wander off by yourself, dear." Enid clenched her jaw. Foolish girl! But how could she know? She relaxed her finger muscles slightly. "Never split the troops."

Sally wrinkled her eyebrow. "I can look after my—"

A faint scraping emanated from the kitchen. Aunt Enid stepped closer, tightened her grip on her walking stick and peered into the dimness. Remnants of street light from the neighbouring back street picked out the vague outlines of benches and cupboards.

The fairy bells tinkled again. Another pungent wave wafted over them, yet the air remained still.

"Stay here," ordered Enid. She snapped on the kitchen light and stepped forward, brandishing her silver walking stick in front of her like a shield. The bead curtain tinkled and chinked as it shivered behind her. The kitchen seemed clear. A kitchen island bench dominated the room. The back door was open - a black gaping maw into the outside world.

A blanket of heat engulfed Enid. She struggled to breathe as it pressed against her chest, almost suffocating her. Her head spun. The heat shimmered and twisted itself away from her. Enid gasped, filling her lungs with air.

"It's just a bloody possum," hissed Sally as she entered the room and stumbled over a few scattered lemon butter jars on the floor. She picked up them up, replaced them in the pantry and closed the door.

The back screen door slapped its frame.

"It's scarpered!" grumped Sally. "It'll be hell to get the smell out."

Enid took a deep breath and examined the kitchen. Several items were scattered across the island bench. An upturned white plastic bottle lay perilously close to the edge of the marble benchtop. A small pyramid of soil, sprinkled with white powder, had been placed on a plastic square next to it. The edges of the powder were stained lavender. A toppled bottle of lemon butter lay in the centre of the bench.

Enid ventured a few steps into the room. She kicked something at her feet. An orange rolled across the tiled floor and bounced off the kick board under the cupboards. Two more jars of lemon butter lay smashed on the ground; their melted contents had already seeped into the grouting of the tiled floor.

Enid's pulse faltered. "Shut the door, Sally." Her voice croaked as she forced out the words and waved Sally around the far side of the kitchen island, away from the mess. Enid leaned across the edge of the stone-topped kitchen island. She flinched; the marble was warm to the touch. She held her breath and peeked over the edge.

Olive's contorted body lay on the floor. Her face was bright-red, with eyes frozen wide - her green irises stood out against the stark white scleras, and her mouth open in a silent scream.

Enid whispered under her breath: "Oh, Olive." Her shoulders slumped.

Olive's clothes were twisted around her body, her blouse skewed to bare her scarlet-skinned shoulder, revealing a faint silver scar in the shape of a crescent. A thin red line circled her throat.

Enid's gaze darted around the kitchen as Sally approached the back door. They were alone. Olive's assailant had fled. They were safe. For now.

She lowered her walking stick, bent down and examined her friend's body. There was no paleness around the lips or eyelids. Her fingernails were pink. She closed Olive's eyes. Her fingers recoiled. The skin was boiling hot. Not cool as expected.

She felt around the body. It *had* to be here. It mustn't fall into— Her fingers tugged on something under Olive's neck. A silver amulet lay wedged under her shoulder, its clasp broken.

She ventured a deep - but ragged - breath, trying to calm her racing heart, and assessed the scene.

Cracked apples and squashed oranges lay amongst strewn shards of blue glass and shattered jars. Lemon butter was smeared across the tiles, disturbed only by a distorted footprint. Spots of green coagulated fluid led across the floor towards the door.

Sally latched the back door, turned back toward Enid. Her eyes widened.

"Oh, my god! Can I help?" She staggered a few steps forward. "Is she—?"

"Dead?" Enid pulled Olive's blouse up to cover her shoulder. "Yes."

Sally placed a gentle hand on Enid's shoulder. "Oh, Aunt Enid, I'm so sorry I doubted you..."

She pulled her mobile phone from her pocket. Her face muscles relaxed, betraying no emotion. It was not the first time Enid had seen her switch into her studied 'professional mode'. She hoped it would be the last.

"Ambulance, please. My great Aunt's friend has collapsed. She's dead." Sally's lips hardened. "Yes, I'm a nurse." She turned away from Enid and continued to talk quickly and quietly.

Enid's heart thumped. She didn't have much time. She examined

Olive's body: broken blood vessels traced down from her neck, over her chest, circled a bruise on her sternum, and continued down under her blouse. Another circular bruise peeked out from under the material. Enid lifted the blouse; there were four bruises in all, each with a blackened edge. Enid brushed a finger over one of the blackened edges and inspected her fingertip. Black. Like soot.

"*And I think someone broke into the house. Yes, I think the police will be a good idea.*" Sally's voice was muffled, barely audible as the blood rushed in Enid's ears. Ice sliced through her veins. Her heart seized. She'd seen such markings before... She reminded herself to breathe. *Sixty years ago.*

Sally clicked her phone off and turned back to Enid. "Police and Ambulance are on their way."

Enid pulled Olive's blouse back over her shoulder, snatched up the amulet and tucked it inside her glove. Sally crouched and reached for Olive's wrist.

"No!" Enid lurched forward. If Sally felt the heat of the body, she'd know something was wrong.

"It's okay, Aunt Enid. I do this for a living. Remember?" She checked for Olive's pulse, then placed the back of her hand on Olive's forehead. She stood up.

Enid touched the skin at Olive's neck. It was cold, as if all the heat had been sucked from her body.

"But, how—?" Enid pulled herself to her feet and leaned on her walking stick.

"There's nothing we could have done." Sally placed her arm around Enid's shoulder. "She's been gone for some time."

"Of course she has. She's cold, dear. Even I know what that means." Enid surprised herself with the crotchety tone of her voice. She extracted herself from Sally's hug, ensured the back door was locked and checked the latch on the kitchen window.

Sirens wailed in the distance.

"We should leave it for the police," Sally placed a gentle hand on Enid's elbow and ushered her out of the kitchen.

Red and blue lights flickered on the door window. Hurried footsteps dashed up the front path and scuffed on the front step. Shadows blotted out the kaleidoscope of lights. There was a knock on the front door.

chapter three

The sweet aroma of baking scones mingled with the tart fragrance of lemon simmering on the stove. A bead of perspiration tickled Enid's nose as she stirred the lemon mixture. A shrill bell pierced the heat. The timer vibrated on the shelf above the wood stove.

Enid slid the saucepan to the back of the stovetop to keep warm, stretched her back and puffed a strand of hair out of her eyes. The first batch of scones was ready.

"Now where's that oven mitt?" she muttered.

The oven door groaned as it opened. A ball of heat escaped, rolled over Enid and dispersed into the far corners of the room. She slid the baking tray onto a wooden board on the bench.

Enid closed her eyes and inhaled the mouth-watering smell of warm butter, vanilla and toasted flour. She felt her shoulder muscles relax, her breathing slowed and calmed her twitching nerves. Baking helped her think, to clear her mind, collect her thoughts and allow solutions to present themselves.

She flipped the switch on the coffee machine. Enid squeezed her eyelids, trying to block the tears. She would not cry. She didn't have time to cry. Her heart sank into her stomach. How could they succeed with only two?

Enid wiped her nose with her sleeve. Poor Olive. Coffee would not suffice. Chocolate. That's what she needed.

She bustled into the pantry, grabbed the large packet of cooking chocolate, and hesitated. A wicked grin flashed over her lips; she reached behind the second box of cocoa and pulled out a packet of dark chocolate chips.

One could never have enough chocolate at times like this.

Enid returned to the bench and took a glass bowl out of the cupboard.

Another timer alarm dinged. Enid dusted her floury fingers on her apron, tapped her fingers on the bases of the upturned glass jars on the drying rack by the sink and took a deep breath.

Mr B yowled and skittered across the linoleum floor, slamming into her leg with a thump.

"What's wrong, Mr B?" Enid leaned down and stroked his back.

He arched his back and pushed against her calf, almost knocking her over. Enid's fingers wrapped around a floury rolling pin as she peered out the window above the sink.

Leaves flitted across the back yard. The gum trees creaked and swayed. Shadows danced across the window. Enid stepped back and sniffed the air. Nothing. Her grip on the rolling pin loosened slightly.

"It's just the wind," she said. "Stop being para--"

The front door rattled. Silence. It rattled again. Enid's other hand reached for a knife on the bench, and she crept down the hall.

There was a knock on the door. Enid's silver walking stick glinted in the umbrella stand. She quietly placed the rolling pin on the hall table and snatched up her trusty stick. No one gets past Enid Turner!

Another knock on the door, this time more insistent. Enid held her breath and raised her walking stick.

"Aunt Enid, are you home?" It was Sally.

Enid dropped her arm beside her body. A ripple of relief flooded through her. She sucked in a deep breath and smiled at the repaired ceramic garden gnome standing on the hall table. Fine cracks traced his features. She patted his hat and whispered to the gnome: "It's all right, Red. It's just Sally."

She hid the kitchen knife in the hall table drawer, slipped the rolling pin into her apron pocket and leaned heavily on her walking stick as she unlatched the door.

"You're early, Sally."

"I thought I'd keep you company until the funeral this afternoon." Sally hugged Enid, glanced back into the garden and closed the door behind her.

Sally was not her usual colourful self - swathed in black, from head to toe. A deep furrow twisted her eyebrows.

"Since when do you lock your door, Aunt Enid?" she asked.

A little white lie would have to suffice. She had to protect her great-niece from the truth.

"Since strangers break into old ladies' houses and scare them to death," said Enid as she slid the door latch home.

"The gnomes are enough to scare them off," mumbled Sally as she dropped her car keys on the hall table next to Red and flinched.

Enid patted Sally's shoulder. "Not when you get to know them."

Sally raised an eyebrow. "I wish they wouldn't paint them with those eyes - you know, like those paintings. They keep staring at me. It gives me the creeps."

Enid bit her lip and winked at Red.

"That's nice, dear." She trotted down the hall towards the kitchen. "You're just in time to help me make a chocolate cake. One can never--"

"--have too much chocolate," finished Sally, with a grin. "I know."

Sally sifted the remaining flour into the bowl, scooped up a spoonful of sour cream and folded it into the mixture.

Aunt Enid screwed the lid closed on the last lemon butter jar, washed her hands and sipped brewed coffee from her teacup. She leaned over the bowl, closed her eyes and took a deep breath. "Perfect. Now fold in the egg whites and--"

"Wouldn't it be quicker to use a cake mix?" asked Sally.

Aunt Enid patted Sally on the shoulder, sat down on a kitchen chair and smiled.

"But much less satisfying, and wouldn't allow me time to think, dear." She slid three buttered cake tins onto the bench next to Sally. "Pop the mix in these."

Sally flipped through her aunt's recipe book. Each page was written in a precise hand and dated at the top of the page. The earliest recipe was written in nib ink, in a similar hand. She glanced at the top of the page: *4th December, 1841.*

Sally raised an eyebrow. "Your ancestors were quite meticulous. Do you still use the original recipes?"

Aunt Enid nodded. "Of course. Mother was an excellent cook." She licked traces of lemon butter from her fingers. "As were her mother and grandmother before her, of course."

Sally flipped through the book. The Devil's Food Cake was dated *23rd September, 1913.* She ran her finger down the recipe's instructions.

"It says a moderate oven."

Aunt Enid pointed to one of the doors on the wood stove. "That one," she said.

Sally's nose twitched. She sniffed the air. Her aunt narrowed her eyelids, peered out the kitchen window and took a deep whiff too. Her eyelids relaxed.

Sally sniffed the air again and frowned. "Do you smell smoke?"

Aunt Enid's eyes widened. "My scones!" She jumped out of her chair, snatched up the oven mitt and threw open the oven. Smoke bled into the room. She coughed, plunged her hands into the oven and pulled out a baking tray of charred scones. She sucked the air in through her teeth and scowled as she dumped them next to the sink. Heat steamed off them in grey wisps as the tray clattered, bounced and skid along the bench, knocking one of the lemon butter jars off the edge.

Aunt Enid spun on her heel and twisted her hand to catch the tumbling jar. Her grey bob flicked over her face as she shuddered to a sudden stop.

Sally's eyes widened. "I wish I had your reflexes."

Her aunt's shoulders drooped. "Adrenalin is an amazing thing." Aunt Enid unlatched the kitchen window. It opened with a squeak.

Sally fanned herself with an empty baking tray. "These old cottages really hold the heat, don't they? I wish you would reconsider moving."

Aunt Enid snatched a tea towel from the rack on the side of the stove. "Turners have lived in this house since eighteen thirty-nine!" She waved the tea towel with both hands, chasing the smoke out the window. "This cottage was rebuilt on the site of our first home. It was the first built in the area, you know?"

It was her aunt's standard reply; she was always reminding her about the history of the family home.

"I know." Sally eyed the insulated wires tracing down the plastered walls, from the ceiling to the round Victorian light switches. "But maybe you could upgrade the electrics? Surely those wires can't be safe?"

"I can look after myself, Sally. I've survived seventy-seven years in this house." Aunt Enid sat down at the kitchen table.

Sally sighed and slumped into the chair beside her. There was no convincing her aunt. She'd lived in the family cottage all her life. The only way to get her to leave would be when she died.

She took a deep breath and surveyed the scene. The side bench was covered in dozens of jars of lemon butter. Scones crowded several wire cooling racks and were stacked in a pyramid on a plate on the table in front of her. Sally's heart sank. She couldn't begin to understand how her aunt must feel - two friends had died in less than a month. She must be missing them terribly.

"That's a lot of scones, Aunt Enid," said Sally. "You've obviously had a lot of thinking to do. The girls at Bingo will never eat them all this afternoon."

"They love scones," replied Aunt Enid. A smile flickered over her lips. "There's some containers in that cupboard." She waved at the wall cupboards. "You pop them in the freezer. I'll put the cake in the oven."

Sally hesitated. "In the laundry?" she asked.

"Yes, where else would it be?"

Sally swallowed. She'd have to brave the horde of garden gnomes in the back yard.

Sally balanced the stack of plastic containers against the wall and tentatively pushed open the back screen door. The smell of eucalyptus wafted on the warm wind. She frowned. The hot change was already on its way. She paused and scanned the yard.

Curved red ceramic cones peeked out of the overgrown grass. A row of garden gnomes lined both sides of the path - all staring at her with those flat, emotionless black eyes...

The screen door slammed behind her. Sally flinched, rolling her foot on the uneven edge of a paver. She jostled to keep the tower of containers upright and thrust her back against the rotary washing line to regain her balance.

The gnomes watched.

Sally shivered. The scones rattled in their containers. She didn't want to hang around here any longer than necessary. She had to get this lot in the freezer. As quickly as possible. She glanced at the red patches in the grass, and scoffed.

Oh, get a grip! They're just statues. Just ignore them and concentrate on getting to the freezer. She held her breath and took a step...

She peered under the containers, checking the position of each step as she edged along the path, then cut across the grass and picked her way past the concealed garden gnomes - never meeting their gaze.

She lifted her gaze and concentrated on the laundry, constructed of sandstone and redbrick quoins matching the main cottage.

Just. One. More. Step.

Sally's lungs felt like they would burst. She gasped for fresh air and balanced the containers on her hip. She fumbled the key in the door lock and wriggled the loose doorknob until she heard its welcome click.

The internal walls were plastered. A large alcove on the opposite side was still home to an ancient, rusty cast-iron stove. This was the original cottage kitchen - almost one-hundred and eighty years old; a gem hidden in the back yard. It was a wonder the local council hadn't noticed it and declared both the old kitchen and the cottage historic buildings.

The wooden floor creaked under Sally's feet as she approached the chest freezer next to the disused stove. The freezer looked decidedly out of place; a massive white metal thing over two metres long, with its lid level with her waist.

Sally's eyes widened. She whistled. "You could hide a body in here!" No one had freezers this big anymore; it was the kind of thing she'd expect a serial killer to have in the shed. Sally shook her head and smiled. Or an over- zealous baker.

She placed the containers on an old rusty tea trolley near the stove and wrenched open the freezer's lid. Chilled air brushed against her face. Inside was packed almost to the brim with containers and freezer bags, their contents barely recognisable through the mortar-like layers of frost.

Sally packed her pile of containers into the chest, squeezing them into available crevices. She wiggled the last one in place and surveyed her work. There was barely room for another baking marathon. She'd have to keep Aunt Enid worry-free until after her next few Bingo nights.

Sally closed the freezer and rubbed her hands to warm the chill in her fingers.

The laundry door knocked against the wall with a thud. Sally's heart leapt into her throat. She spun on her heel.

Aunt Enid stood in the doorway, dressed in a smart black dress and small black hat, and fussed with her gloves.

"Come on, Sally. We don't want to be late for the funeral."

chapter four

O live would have been happy; the funeral service had been short, but well attended. Her friends had farewelled her in style, their numbers making up for lack of family members. One notable absence was her grandson. Enid wiped away a tear. Olive was a dear friend, not easy to replace.

Agnes had been there - and most of the grey brigade from Bingo. Mr Knowles had sat behind her, having appointed himself her personal carer for the day, determined to ensure she was not distressed.

Sally had shadowed Enid all day. She was a good girl; she'd dutifully accompanied her old aunt to the funeral, transported a boot-full of scones, provided moral support at the wake, and offered to whisk her away and drive her up the Hill to give Olive a private farewell.

The car engine coughed as it turned into the cemetery road. Ghost gums leaned toward them, casting long shadows in the afternoon light. Dust eddies shimmered in the heat rising off the bitumen. Enid readjusted the air conditioning vent; the returning heat wave had blanketed the city, its fingers creeping into the Hills during the afternoon.

Enid eyed Sally. She had claimed immunity to the shock of discovering a dead body; having seen it all before at work. Still, it had been good for her to attend the funeral; everyone needs closure in such situations. Even nurses.

"Thank you for driving me today, Sally." Enid patted Sally's hand. "I appreciate the company."

"That's okay, Aunt Enid." Sally flashed a smile. "I don't think I could've eaten one more scone." She rolled her eyes.

The dashboard rattled as the car left the bitumen road.

"It doesn't look like anyone else has come to pay their respects," said Sally.

The wheels of the car ground to a halt in the gravel car park next to a big blue trailer. Enid glanced at the gold lettering: *Simon Oldham's Gardening Services*.

Sally turned off the engine.

"I wouldn't say that." Dust tickled Enid's nostrils as she opened the car door. "It looks like Olive's grandson is here. He seems like a good boy. I was thinking of having him take a look at my hydrangeas."

A conspiracy of ravens fidgeted in the trees along the cemetery fence line, outside the stone wall. They circled above, their shadows rippling over the uneven gravel, as Enid and Sally walked toward the stone archway entrance, then turned in the opposite direction and flew back to the sanctuary of the eucalyptus gum and native pine trees.

Gravel crunched under Enid and Sally's feet as they strolled along the bare track curving through the ageing heart of the cemetery. Ornately carved sandstone and marble headstones rose from beds of dry earth, like chiselled diaries, chronicling the lives - and deaths - of the slumbering residents to any who knew how to transcribe their code.

Flaking slate grave markers, with names long erased by the elements, betrayed earlier, forgotten graves. Fashionable, carved stone pillars with weathered epitaphs, enclosed within wrought-iron enclosures of packed gravel, singled out the affluent in a profusion of more austere monuments. Later generations boasted ornate carved marble monuments, many now cracked with age and pockmarked with drilled holes where brass lettering had once been attached.

They trudged onward. Scattered tufts of dry grass multiplied. Dry, dusty ground gave way to green grass, leading down the hill to the clipped lawn and rows of polished black marble headstones occupying the newest section of the cemetery.

Metal scraped on hard ground. The sound grew louder as they continued toward the copse of evergreen trees at the edge of the old section of the cemetery. Something moved in the shade under the trees.

"We're a bit early." Enid halted. "It looks like young Simon is still paying his respects."

"Is that where...?" whispered Sally.

Enid nodded. The last resting place of her dear friend, and colleague, Olive Oldham.

"Oh." Sally lowered her eyes and wandered toward a group of assorted headstones enclosed in a low cement border.

Enid closed her eyes and let the warm wind caress her face. She could almost hear Olive's wicked chuckle as she crossed off a winning Bingo number, her triumphant sigh after a task completed, and her gasp when pleasantly surprised.

"Edith Anne Turner. Born 1807. Died 1839." Sally gasped quietly.

Enid opened her eyes.

Sally smiled and glanced along the enclosure towards the older stone grave markers. "Mary Elizabeth Turner. Died: 1918." Gravel scrunched under her feet as she stepped closer to a cracked, grey marble headstone. "Archibald William Turner... Died: 1862." Her eyes widened. "Is this our Turners?" she asked. "Do we have a family plot?"

Enid nodded.

Thunder rumbled in the distance. A hot wind eddy clawed at the dirt track and tugged at Enid's skirt. Shadows fluttered in the corner of Enid's vision. She scanned the darkening clouds.

Not now!

"Will you be buried here when--?" Sally's face reddened.

"Yes," replied Enid. "And you, too, if you so desire."

Sally frowned. "I hadn't thought of that."

The scrape of a shovel echoed through the grounds and ricocheted off the headstones. Enid peered into the shadows. A lone figure piled dirt onto a small mound next to an iron-fenced headstone. Enid raised an eyebrow. Not Olive's grandson.

Sally glanced at the busy workman under the trees. "I suppose we all have to go one day, but I wouldn't want to live forever."

Enid's heart sank. She turned away from the enclosure. "It is usually the case," she whispered.

Sally spun on her heel. "I... I..." A furrow deepened between her eyebrows as she frowned. She reached her hand out toward Enid and shook her head slowly. "I'm sorry, Aunt Enid."

Sally's gentle hand touched Enid's shoulder. Enid clenched her hand, gripping her walking stick until her knuckles paled, and swallowed a curse.

"I didn't mean..." said Sally.

Enid held her breath. She had to relax. She couldn't let Sally know. Not yet. She uncurled her fingers. "I know, Sally."

A crack echoed over the cemetery. The ground shivered faintly under Enid's feet. She blinked as the gravedigger slammed his mallet on a pale wooden marker again and again.

Enid leaned on her walking stick. Olive was gone. How could she and Agnes continue alone?

Shadows turned in the air above the car park. The ravens circled and settled on the perimeter wall but continued to protest.

The gravedigger collected his shovel and mallet, slapped on his hat and trekked back down to the shed at the bottom of the hill. His tools bounced and rattled in the wheelbarrow as it skittered and rumbled along the uneven gravel road.

Dark clouds gathered above the tree line. The air smelled of ozone, but was as dry as the gravel. There was no moisture, no promised alleviation to the oppressive heat.

"He's finished," whispered Enid. "We best pay our respects. There's a storm brewing."

It was slightly cooler in the shade of the old trees. Their leaves rustled as they caught the wind and diverted it along the track. A veil of dust hung in the air and caught in the back of Enid's throat with each breath.

A grave marker lay broken against an exposed tree root. Its bottom half, lifted partially out of the ground, tilted at an awkward angle. Thin scrollwork traced its edges. Drill holes scarred the marble where the patina-ed brass lettering had been removed or fallen away, though the inscription was still visible as weathered shadows

Sally read the inscription:

"Frederick Joseph Oldham. Born 1842.
Died 1888.
Beloved husband of--"

Her shoulders drooped. "Oh, it's broken along the inscription."

They circled the grave's wrought-iron fence. A mound of dry earth marked Olive's freshly filled grave. A white wooden cross stood as a temporary place marker at the far end. Delicate bunches of lavender were painted on each arm of the cross. The posies' black painted ribbons entwined around Olive's hand-painted epitaph:

Olive Ruby Oldham.
Died 2018.

"That's strange. There's no date of birth," said Sally.

"Perhaps there wasn't room?"

"But--"

"And Olive never liked to admit her age."

Ravens twitched on the fence. A lone bird gargled its song, the last note lowering as if in mournful melancholy.

Enid's chin quivered. She would miss Olive. How could she ever be replaced?

Lightning lit up the sky. Clouds crackled with light. Another peal of thunder rumbled down from the North. Enid peered into the sky.

Not now!

Shadows crept around the tree. The leaves shook furiously as the wind changed direction and roared between the branches.

Gravel crunched on the other side of the tree copse. A lone figure trudged along the track, hands stuffed in his jeans pocket. Tufts of ginger hair poked out from under the hood of his jacket.

Sally turned and watched him continue along the road toward the car park. "Is that her grandson?"

Enid examined the man's face: angled nose, strong chin, piercing blue eyes. She smiled. He looked like his grandfather. "It must be," she whispered.

"You know, he's kind of cute." Sally stared after him as he crossed under the arched entrance.

Thunder rumbled through the sky. A silver fissure fractured the sky several feet above Enid's head. The fissure extended, slicing through the air. It shimmered and crackled as it widened.

Enid froze. She glanced in Sally's direction. She was still distracted by Olive's grandson, seemingly oblivious to what she must have thought was 'just another' lightning storm. Why not? They were common enough in summer. But this was not just another--

The centre of the fissure darkened.

The ravens cawed. Their wings spread and beat the air as they rose from the fence and flapped back into the trees surrounding the car park. The trees shuddered under their weight.

The clouds darkened and coalesced above them. A shadow crept in from the entrance, and rippled along the gravel road, closer to Sally.

Enid's heart cramped. Her hand clasped her blouse at her throat.

Not here. Not now.

She straightened her back, pulled back her shoulders and stabbed the tip of her walking stick into the air, clenching it until her knuckles paled.

She mumbled under her breath: "*Claudere porta.*"

"Pardon? Did you say something, Aunt Enid?" Sally turned back to face Enid.

Enid's hand dropped back to her side.

The air rumbled.

The trailer bounced and squeaked off along Cemetery Road.

The fissure crackled. Its light flickered and glistened in the polished silver of Enid's walking stick. Then it fizzled and snapped shut with a loud crack.

Sally jumped. "That was a close one!"

Enid leaned on her walking stick. "I'm tired, dear. It's been a long day." Her mind raced; how dare they? And in a place of rest. It was neutral. Forbidden! Even they knew that. Was nowhere sacred - nowhere safe - anymore?

Enid's gaze skittered across the sky, over the headstones, along the road and toward the entrance. All was clear. But for how long?

She slipped her arm around Sally's elbow and led her back along the gravel track, past Mary Elizabeth, past Edith Anne. She nodded in Archibald's direction and lowered her eyes.

I'm sorry. It won't happen again.

A lone raven flew down and landed on top of the entrance arch. It blinked; its gaze followed Enid as she ushered Sally to the car. It cawed as they climbed inside. It glided across the car park and landed quietly on the hood of the car.

"I know," whispered Enid. She rubbed the neck of her blouse. She could feel the metal of her amulet under the black linen.

"Pardon?" Sally slipped the key into the ignition.

"I have something for you." Enid fumbled in her purse.

Sally eyed the purse.

"It's a family heirloom."

"No, Aunt Enid." Sally placed her hand on Enid's wrist, staying it. "That's not why I visit you."

"But I want to, dear. It'll make me happy. And I'm not getting any younger." She pulled Olive's circular amulet from her purse. The clasp had been repaired, and the silver was polished, highlighting the sapphire at its centre.

She pressed the amulet into Sally's palm, and held her breath. The sapphire glinted; the chain fell and slithered down into Sally's hand.

Enid let out her breath and smiled. "Think of it as a good luck charm."

Sally held it up to the light. The amulet turned slowly in the air, the blue light reflected in Sally's eyes as her gaze followed each revolution.

"It's beautiful," she whispered. "But I can't--"

"It's time to pass it on," said Enid.

Sally grinned and looped the chain around her neck. Enid's amulet warmed the skin under her blouse.

Rain dripped on the roof of the car. The raven inclined its head and lifted into the air. It circled the car and landed in one of the trees lining the car park.

Enid snapped shut her bag, closed her eyes and sighed.

Sally was safe.

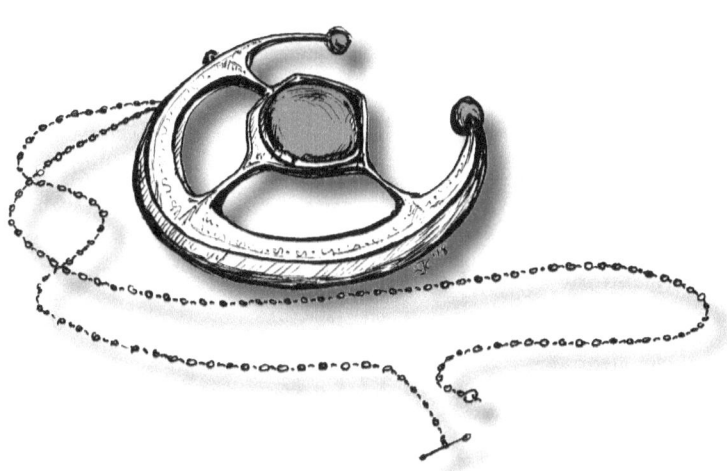

chapter five

soft murmur filled the Bingo hall. Silver-haired seniors huddled together and whispered condolences. Enid had allowed Agnes to drag her along to Bingo to cheer up. She settled into her regular chair. A collective sigh rippled over the usually jocular crowd.

The urn simmered and bubbled. A trickle of steam escaped from the top. Plates of cakes, tarts and scones sat untouched on the trestle table next to it.

She surveyed the rest of the hall. Heads nodded and eyes flickered a sombre greeting in her direction. Enid sighed; there wasn't a smile in the hall. Not one. Every eye was either red-rimmed, tear-infused, or drooping in pity. Her shoulders slumped; there would be no jolly taunts nor flirtatious coveting of baked goods tonight.

She forced a weak smile, nodded in response and busied herself squaring up her Bingo cards.

"A gift from Mr Knowles." Agnes grinned and placed a teacup on the table in front of Enid.

The china cup rattled quietly on its saucer. Steam curled off the hot liquid.

"How are you coping?" asked Agnes. She placed a gentle hand on Enid's, and squeezed it gently. Comforting warmth seeped into her skin.

"Better than this lot." Enid sipped the coffee. She closed her eyes and allowed her muscles to relax.

"Death is only sorrow to those who fear it," whispered Agnes.

Enid opened her eyelid a crack, and eyed her friend; that was insightful for young Agnes.

Enid glanced at the vacant chair beside her. "I miss her, Agnes."

"I know." Agnes sat in the chair next to Enid and lowered her voice. "Was it a Collector?"

Enid nodded. "I saw the markings. I don't think it was after her soul."

Agnes' eyes widened. "It tried to infiltrate her?" She swallowed. "They haven't attempted that in—"

"Sixty years. I know. I checked *The Books*."

"So, they are collecting again." Agnes shifted in her chair. "They're going to try to break through, aren't they?"

"They already have. In the cemetery," replied Enid.

Agnes flinched. Her chair scraped on the polished floorboards. "But that's... it's against the rules."

"Since when has The Dark cared about rules?"

"At least it didn't add Olive to the tally," replied Agnes.

Enid turned the teacup on its saucer.

"How can you be so calm, Enid?" Agnes leaned in close and spoke in a strained whisper. "They attacked Olive! How? We should have been warned. Surely all her Wards were in place?"

"It would have had to fool the Wards." Enid leaned back in her chair. She tried to recall the earlier entries in *The Books*. She swallowed another mouthful of coffee; caffeine usually helped jog her memory. There *was* something...

"There was one time... A Collector infiltrated a host and used it like a protective armour of skin."

Agnes wrinkled her nose.

Enid held her cup of coffee under her nose, breathed in the fumes and let the aroma linger.

"There was an incident, in the sixties? Or was it the twenties?" Enid shook her head. "Oh, my memory isn't what it was. I think it's time to consult *The Books*."

Agnes leaned her elbow on the table and bit her thumbnail. "Has The Dark ever come close to collecting its allotment of souls?"

"Not for generations."

"And this time it seems to be after us." Agnes swallowed. "That means you're not safe." Her gaze darted around the hall. "I'm not safe."

The hall clock chimed seven. The seniors shuffled to their seats. Mr Knowles sidled up close to Enid.

"May I join you, Miss Turner?" he asked.

Enid gathered up her pencils from the table and sighed. The poor man just couldn't take a hint. She'd have to let him down gently.

"Of course, Mr Knowles." Agnes beamed and nudged Enid under the table.

"Call me Alfred."

"Thank you, Alfred. You must call me Agnes. And this is Enid."

Enid glared at Agnes - ever the matchmaker.

"I hope I wasn't interrupting?" he asked.

"No, we were just talking about... Olive," replied Agnes.

Mr Knowles glanced at the empty seat on the other side of Enid and removed his hat.

"My condolences, Miss—." He smiled and cleared his throat. "Enid."

Enid opened her mouth to object, but was cut short by a swift kick to the shin under the table. She glared at Agnes again.

"I meant to offer them after the funeral but I missed you."

"I had to leave early. My niece had to go to work." It was only a little white lie. And how would he ever find out?

Mr Knowles lowered his eyes and crumpled the brim of his hat.

"Yes, the poor girl. She was with you when you found...?" His voice trailed off.

"She's all right," replied Enid. "Sally's a nurse. She's seen death before. I dare say she's more accustomed to it than you, Mr Knowles."

Mr Knowles raised an eyebrow.

"I'm sorry, Alfred," said Agnes. "Enid is not herself tonight."

There was a long, uncomfortable silence. Enid fidgeted with the pencils in her hand. Mr Knowles rocked on his heels and examined the lining of his hat. Agnes rolled her eyes. Finally, Agnes cleared her throat.

"I'm thinking of hiring a gardener," said Agnes.

Enid stopped fidgeting. "I've hired Olive's grandson, Simon. He's coming over to look at my garden next week. I can ask him if he's looking for more work."

Agnes raised an eyebrow. "Didn't he work on Olive's garden?"

Enid nodded.

"But you said Olive's garden was half-dead."

"Oh, the rest of the garden was *immaculate*. It was just the—" Enid sucked in a breath. The hydrangeas! She leaned close to Agnes and whispered in her ear. "What kind of intruder only destroys the hydrangeas?"

Agnes' eyes widened.

"There wasn't an intruder," said Mr Knowles as she checked his Bingo cards.

"No intruder?" Enid spun to face him. "How do you know?"

"They say she left the back door unlocked," he replied.

"Who says?" asked Enid. "Agnes *never* left the door unlocked."

"That's true. She was the most careful of us all," added Agnes.

"I suppose the police will discover their error during their investigation," said Enid.

Mr Knowles shook his head. "They aren't conducting an investigation."

"Why ever not?" Enid asked.

"They don't consider your friend's death to be suspicious," replied Mr Knowles. "The Coroner said it was a heart attack."

"Heart attack, my arse!" grumbled Enid. Hadn't they seen the scorch marks on Olive's chest? She couldn't do that to herself.

The hall went quiet.

The Bingo Caller cleared his throat and tapped his microphone. "I can see Miss Turner is eager to start. So, pencils ready, ladies and gentlemen."

One of the pencils slipped from her hand and clattered on the table.

Mr Knowles caught the pencil and handed it back to Enid.

Agnes patted Enid on her arm. "People are watching, Enid." She turned to Mr Knowles. "Alfred, I think Enid needs another cup of coffee."

"I don't need another cup of coffee, Agnes," whispered Enid through clenched teeth.

"I'm sure Alfred is only trying to help." Agnes waved and nodded in the Caller's direction.

"Excellent, let's begin. The first number is..." His voice droned into the background.

Enid sucked in a deep breath and lowered her voice: "And how exactly do you know there's no police investigation, Mr Knowles?"

"My son works at the local police station."

"Really?" asked Enid.

"Yes, he's a detective." Mr Knowles' chest puffed with pride.

Enid placed her pencils on the table, next to her stack of Bingo cards.

"Why don't you sit down, Alfred?" asked Agnes.

He stood behind the remaining empty chair next to Enid, and hesitated.

Agnes slid over, vacating her chair on the other side of Enid. She patted her empty seat. "Sit down, Alfred."

"So..." Enid toyed with her collection of pencils as Albert sat down. "If we found some evidence to prove suspicious circumstances, your son would be the one to inform?"

"I suppose, but—"

"Then we need to prove the Police wrong, there was an intruder and Olive's death was foul play." She sipped the last of her coffee and smiled. "I suppose the Police didn't even bother to do a - what do they call it on the television - a door knock - to see if anyone saw anything untoward?" asked Enid.

Alfred shrugged. "You'd have to ask my son, Tom."

Enid grinned. "I have an assignment for you. I would consider it a great personal favour..."

"Enid, don't put him on the spot like that," whispered Agnes.

Enid ignored her protest. "I'm sure you can be very persuasive, Alfred." She sidled her chair a little closer. "It appears we shall have to do the Police's work for them. I need you to find out if anyone saw anything unusual near Olive's house on the day she died."

Agnes' eyes widened. She shook her head slowly.

Alfred nodded. "I'm your man." He paused, flipped over a Bingo card and drew columns on the back. "But finding a suspect is not enough," he continued, "Tom always says there are three things they need: means, motive and opportunity." He spoke quickly, barely pausing for a breath. "If someone was there, we could argue opportunity, but what about means and motive? What was the motive? Did your friend have valuables?" He tapped his pencil. "And how could a killer make a death look like a heart attack?"

He scribbled down notes on the card. Enid and Agnes stared at each other, their mouths open.

Agnes mouthed: *What have you done?*

Enid shrugged. These were all good questions, but how could they tell him the truth: the suspect they were looking for was a supernatural force from an alternate world?

Alfred looked up from his notes. "This is just like an Agatha Christie novel." There was a definite sparkle in his eyes.

"I prefer Sherlock Holmes, myself," said Enid.

Agnes sighed. "Oh, Arthur was *such* a nice man."

Alfred lifted his pencil from the card and turned to Agnes. "He would have died before you were born, wouldn't he?"

Enid glared at Agnes, and put her finger to her lips. Agnes bit her lip.

"Um... Agnes means that, having read his books, she feels like she knows him."

Agnes nodded. A little too quickly.

"Ah." Alfred nodded and returned to his note making.

Enid scowled at Agnes. She was never one for discretion.

"I could ask Tom about the postmortem report," he mumbled. "I've got my list. Ladies, may I suggest you check your friend's house for clues and we can compare notes when we're done."

Agnes frowned. "Perhaps, we should leave it to the police, Enid?"

"Nonsense." Alfred scoffed.

"Then it's settled," said Enid. She had unleashed Alfred's 'inner sleuth'. It seemed there was no stopping him now. "Alfred, you check for witnesses. Agnes, you assist me at the house, and I'll talk to Olive's bees to find out if they noticed anything."

"Bees?" Alfred turned to her.

"Of course, dear." Enid sighed. "Bees know everything."

"Bingo!"

Enid shoved her Bingo cards aside. Alfred, dropped his pen, cracked his knuckles and rose from his chair. "Another cup of coffee?" he asked.

Enid and Agnes both nodded.

"Excellent." Alfred swaggered over to the side table.

Agnes grabbed Enid's sleeve and dragged her onto the chair Alfred had been sitting in. "What are you doing, Enid?" she hissed.

"The sooner we can discover the identity of the infiltrated host, the quicker we can track down The Dark's next victim. If we can't yet use the local police to our advantage, why deny a willing assistant? 'All hands on deck' as my father used to say."

"But we can't risk a civilian!" She strained to keep from being overheard by the next table.

"It's our duty to protect this world, Agnes." Enid looked her directly in the eye. "Whatever the cost."

"Is that why you gave Olive's amulet to Sally? You would risk your own blood, and make her one of us? What will you tell her? Daemons, fairies and magic are all real?"

Enid caught her breath. She already felt guilty about involving Sally. She didn't need Agnes to fuel the fire.

"She will think you're going dotty." Agnes' grip tightened. "Trust me, most people prefer to have a say in their own fate. They don't take kindly to being manipulated into one."

Enid didn't answer. She closed her eyes and took a deep breath. Agnes was correct; how could she explain? She had thought she was protecting Sally with the amulet; she'd never even considered the consequences. She dug her nails into the palm of her hand. *What had she done?*

Enid sat between Agnes and Alfred, and sipped her coffee. It was perfect - sweetened with honey, not sugar. Alfred had remembered she preferred it that way.

"Legs eleven." The Bingo Caller grinned.

"I didn't think anyone said that any more," said Enid.

"He's new. Thinks he's a game show host," said Alfred.

"Bingo!" A woman on the table in front of them jumped to her feet.

Everyone cheered. Agnes clapped enthusiastically.

"I say, we're taking this whole situation very lightly." Alfred wrung the brim of his hat. "You do realise that, *if* there was an intruder, your niece was there with you. Perhaps she saw something you didn't? Perhaps you should ask her as well?"

Enid's heart froze.

Her skin tingled. She touched the amulet around her neck. It felt warm. She glanced at Agnes. Did she feel it too?

Agnes showed no sign of alarm. Her gaze swung between Enid and Alfred. A smile flickered over her lips. She was matchmaking again. Enid dropped her hand from the amulet. Perhaps she was mistaken?

Enid's chest burned. Her stomach lurched. She *wasn't* mistaken. She packed away her pencils and turned to Agnes.

"Sally's not safe. We need to warn her," she whispered in Agnes' ear, so Alfred could not hear.

Agnes' smile dropped. She crossed out the number on her card. "But I've only got a few more numbers to go."

"We've got to go, Agnes." Enid's chair scraped as she stood.

The Caller's microphone screeched. "Is that 'Bingo', Miss Turner?" he asked.

Enid shook her head and waved him on.

"Very well, let's continue." He reached into the basket and pulled out another number.

"Now, Agnes." There was steel in Enid's voice as she dropped her hand on Agnes' shoulder, and handed her Bingo cards to Alfred.

"Duty calls, I'm afraid, Alfred."

Alfred nodded. "Keen to start sleuthing, eh?"

"Something like that," replied Enid.

"Then let me escort you," He pulled his car keys from his pocket.

"Thank you, Alfred." Enid flashed him a warm smile. "But Agnes has already offered me a lift."

Alfred's shoulder dropped. "Very well. I'll contact you when my mission is complete."

Enid smiled. "Alfred, you are a gem."

chapter six

Sally opened the window. A hot breeze swirled around her kitchen. The current heat wave had dragged on since Mrs Oldham's funeral. She wiped her forehead, poured herself a lemon iced tea and eyed the plastic cake container on the bench top. She unsealed the cake container and inhaled. The rich aroma of dark chocolate filled her lungs.

She licked her lips. Aunt Enid knew her weakness all too well. She resealed the container, patted the lid and grinned. The cake would have to wait until after dinner.

Sally pressed a knob on the stovetop. Gas flames popped into life. The lamb chops sizzled in the frying pan as she rummaged in the crisper drawer for the salad.

Thumps filtered down the hall from the direction of the lounge room. Sally frowned. She was certain she'd switched off the television. She peered into the lounge room. The screen was black, the room silent. She shook her head and returned to the kitchen.

The chops crackled. Sally reached for a pair of metal tongs and turned the meat.

Shadowy reflections flickered in the stainless steel range hood above the stove. Sally flinched, and spun on her heel to face the window. There was nothing there.

The curtains flapped in the wind. Sally's heart leapt into her throat. Her fingers curled around a mug on the bench.

Still nothing. She scoffed. *Why are you so jumpy, Sally?*

She yanked the window shut, straightened the curtains and edged toward the back door. The screen door was locked. She hesitated, shut the back door with a click, and checked the deadlock. *Still... Can't be too cautious.*

The meat popped on the stovetop. A whiff of smoke curled up from the pan. Sally turned the chops over; the meat had crisped in her neglect. She flicked on the rangehood to allow the smoke to escape.

A trickle of sweat slithered down her forehead. She pulled a tea towel off the rack and fanned herself. She must be daft to cook a meal in this heat. What was she thinking?

Sally leaned across the sink to reopen the window. Her fingers froze midair, remembering Mrs Oldham's fate: found dead in her own kitchen. Sally's fingers tensed. Best leave it shut.

She leaned against the sink and scanned the kitchen. Other than a desperate need to wash the dishes, everything was in its place. Everything was normal. So why did she have this uneasy feeling she was being watched?

Sally flexed her fingers, returned the tea towel to its drying rail and turned her attention back to the frying pan.

Something tapped, rolled across the tiled floor and nudged Sally's foot. She watched the apple rebound and bump into a cupboard.

Sally sucked in a breath of hot air. Her chest tightened. Her lungs cramped.

She leaned against the bench. Her fingers twitched as she searched for the drawer handle behind her. It slid open effortlessly. Her fingers curled around the handle of a carving knife. With a nudge of her hip, the drawer closed silently on its automatic runners.

She stepped forward - or tried to - but the hem of her top caught, with a faint rip. She tugged at the material. It was caught tight.

There was another faint rip. This time it wasn't her top.

Sally froze and scanned the room.

The chops crackled.

She was alone.

Oh, this was ridiculous! There was nothing in the room; she turned to extricate herself from the drawer.

The necklace Aunt Enid gave her warmed on her chest. Her ears thrummed as the air pressure rose. A hot shiver ran up her spine, pricking the hair on her neck. She spun on her heel and thrust the knife out in front of her, into empty space.

Still nothing. Sally relaxed. It was just her imagination.

The smell of ozone mingled with that of burning meat and smoke... She screwed up her nose. And something more pungent.

The air prickled again. Pain crushed Sally's chest - as if all the oxygen had been sucked out of the air; she struggled to breathe.

Something brushed against her arm. Searing heat bored deep into her shoulder. She twisted in agony. Her heart raced. Her hand swung out blindly, slashing the vacant air with the carving knife. Heat scorched the base of her neck.

Again, the pain sliced Sally's shoulder, so fast her stomach churned and her head spun. She staggered back, her hands flailing, trying to find something - anything - to hold, to regain her balance.

The frying pan clattered to the floor. Flecks of pain pricked her calves. The smell of burned meat enveloped her. Sally gagged, trying to keep the contents of her stomach from rising.

Gas flickered on the burner. A sweltering blast of heat swirled through the kitchen. It tugged at the curtains and wrenched the tea towels from their rail.

Sally snatched at the cloth as it twisted through the air toward the now-towering blue flames issuing from the stovetop. Tea towels fluttered onto the stove. Orange flames erupted mid-air.

She retreated to the back door and jiggled the lock. The deadlock didn't move. She was trapped.

Her heart contorted in her chest. She gulped in a mouthful of heated air. Her lungs ached. She spluttered as she peered through the thickening haze looking for a means of escape. Perhaps the window above the sink?

The window shuddered and flung open. The fly screen shook and rattled in its frame. The curtains smouldered. Their corners flared. Red rivulets crept along the weave. Chunks of material detached and fluttered to the ground. Finally, the flames caught hold and licked the ceiling.

Perhaps she could make a dash for the hallway?

A roar of wind rushed out the window, sucking part of the smoke across the room along with it.

Sally's eyes stung. Her vision blurred. Scorching air burnt down her trachea and seared her lungs. Blood reverberated through her ears. And the room went dark.

Agnes' burgundy-coloured Wolseley raced along the road. Street lights flickered across the polished wooden dash. The amulet around Enid's neck stung against her skin. Enid craned her head past Agnes' arm to the check the speedometer.

"Can't this old rust bucket go any faster?" she grumbled.

The traffic light glowed red. Agnes slowed the car to a stop.

"Bessie's not a rust bucket," snapped Agnes as she wrestled with the gears on the steering wheel column. "I'll have you know, she got 'Best Original' at the last year's Classic Car Show."

The indicator clicked.

"Besides, I've only got a few points left on my license. If I lose it, you won't have anyone to drive you to Bingo."

The traffic light changed; the green glow cast through the car made the burgundy vinyl car seats appear black as night. Agnes turned the car into Sally's street.

Enid's amulet grew hotter. "Hurry up, Agnes. Something is not right." She gripped the amulet at her neck. "Can't you feel it?"

Agnes frowned. "It could be a false alarm."

The streetlight in front of Sally's house was dark, leaving the house in shadow. Enid peered into the darkness and reached for the door handle.

Agnes grabbed her elbow. "Not yet, Enid. We haven't stopped." She eyed the dead streetlight as she parked the car. "That's not a good sign."

"No, it's not." Enid ripped off her seat belt and sprang out of the car, her silver walking stick waggling in her hand, and rushed to the front door.

A high-pitched alarm squealed at the back of the house.

"Enid, look!" Agnes stood frozen by the car - mouth gaping - and pointed to the sky above the roofline.

Smoke curled from the back of the house. Enid's heart leapt in her chest.

"Sally!" She thumped on the front door as she peered through the window. Shadows flickered at the end of the hall. "Not my Sally, you don't." She strained to remain calm. "Call the fire brigade, Agnes."

The back door rattled in the distance. The amulet burned Enid's skin. Her heart froze.

"Sally, get out of the house!" She growled in frustration and raced along the side driveway toward the back of the house.

Agnes' hurried footsteps followed.

A crack reverberated down the side of the house. Glass shattered.

"I'm coming, Sally!" Enid's pace quickened.

Enid was the first to reach the kitchen door. Smoke trickled out from under it. Orange light flickered through the curtains of the back window. The air shuddered and roared, knocking Enid off-balance.

Agnes staggered up to the door beside her.

Black smoke poured out of the kitchen window and rushed skyward. It writhed in the heat of the flames. Two red eyes glowed in its heart. They turned to face the two women and flared brighter.

The air shuddered again. A thunderous flapping buffeted Enid and tousled her hair. She leaned into the whirlwind and refused to give ground.

"No, you don't!" She thrust her walking stick into the air. The silver glowed in the darkness. "This time you have to deal with *two* of us," she hissed.

Wood cracked and splintered in the darkness. The kitchen door flung open and slammed against the wall. Light spilled into the back yard.

The Collector wobbled. Its eyes flared; it roared in rage and streaked off into the night, extinguishing streetlights in its wake.

Enid lowered her walking stick and rushed into the kitchen

"Sally?"

Sally moaned on the tiled floor.

Flames licked the tiled roof. Thick smoke engulfed the back yard. The house fire alarm pierced Enid's eardrums. Sirens raced toward them, cutting out when the emergency vehicles turned into the street. Agnes waited at the front of the car and waved down the ambulance.

Sally perched on the edge of the passenger seat of the old Wolseley, her feet resting in the gutter, and gasped for fresh air.

"Can't someone turn off that noise?" Sally whispered groggily.

The ambulance pulled up to the curb just before the fire engine. Splashes of red and blue light danced across the pale brick facade of Sally's house. Two sets of respondents jumped from the vehicles. Two men, in heavy golden yellow Turnout coats, jogged toward the house, dragging a fire hose behind them. The other two, in dark green jumpsuits, strode towards the car.

The female Ambulance Officer glanced at Sally and motioned to her partner. His paramedic case clattered on the footpath beside the car.

"Hello." The woman nodded in the direction of the smoke and flames. "Was she inside?" she asked Enid.

Enid nodded.

"Do you know how long?"

Enid shook her head and frowned. "But she was barely conscious when we found her."

The male ambulance officer flashed a pen torch into Sally's eyes. She glared at him and leaned back into the car. He shrugged and placed the torch back in his box.

"She doesn't like people fussing over her," Enid advised him. "She's a nurse; she's used to being in charge."

"I need to check your oxygen levels, okay?" He smiled at Sally.

Sally reached out her hand, winced and jerked backward. She pulled at the collar of her blouse, her face contorted in pain.

The man frowned and eyed Sally. "Can I take a look?" he asked.

Sally nodded.

He carefully unbuttoned the top of her blouse. An angry, red crescent-shaped mark was burnt into her skin.

Enid gasped.

"It's all right." The woman smiled at Enid. "We'll look after her." She opened another section of the paramedic box and turned her attention to Sally.

Enid tugged at Agnes' sleeve. "It was a Collector," she whispered in Agnes' ear.

Agnes' eyes widened. "Are you sure? A Collector? *Here?*"

Enid ushered her further down the footpath, away from the commotion.

"Didn't you feel it? The amulet's warning?" asked Enid.

"Perhaps a little. I was..." Agnes bit her lip.

"Too busy matchmaking," Enid hissed. "And *you* scold *me* - you, who never takes the calling seriously. This isn't a game, Agnes. You should know that by now."

Agnes lowered her gaze. "I never wanted this."

Enid took a deep breath. "I know." She wrapped her arm around Agnes' shoulders. "But now isn't the time for recriminations. We have a—"

"Duty to save the innocent."

Enid felt Agnes' shoulder slump under her arm.

"And right now that duty is to protect Sally," she said.

Agnes raised her eyes. "From being collected?"

"Or infiltrated," replied Enid.

Agnes frowned. "Pardon?"

"You saw the mark." Enid's voice was slow and measured.

Agnes sucked in a breath. Her hand went to her chest. "But she has Olive's amulet. It will protect her."

"It didn't protect Olive," said Enid. "And she had years of experience."

Agnes went pale.

"The Dark is cunning. It won't make the same mistake again," said Enid. "It will give its Collector new orders. Its lieutenants are loyal - and relentless."

She glanced back at her great niece. Sally now sat in the back of the ambulance, a bandage taped to her chest and an oxygen mask over her face. Enid's heart felt as if it was being ripped from her chest. This was all her fault. She should have never given her the amulet. She knew nothing of The Dark or the Collectors.

"It's been over a week. The Collector will have a new host by now. It needs a new host - a body - if it's to collect more souls. I should have warned her." Enid twisted her walking stick into the ground.

"Perhaps we should tell her?" whispered Agnes.

"No, you said it yourself: I can't force this - us - on her. I need to keep her safe, protect her from the Collectors."

Agnes glanced up at the sky and swallowed.

"It already has Sally's scent," replied Enid, "from when we found Olive." Enid's hand trembled. "I need to keep her safe from the Collectors."

Agnes patted her shoulder. "It's not your fault, Enid. How could you have known?"

Enid rolled her shoulder back, away from Agnes' touch. "We should have known. It's our responsibility."

"I won't let it hurt her," said Agnes, still eyeing the night sky. "But promise me you won't tell her yet, Enid. She needs to understand..."

Enid glared at her friend.

"Use your logic, Enid." Agnes grasped Enid's forearm. "You'll have a hard time fulfilling your responsibilities from a locked room in the dementia ward."

Enid twisted from Agnes' grip and rubbed her arm. She passed Agnes, trying to focus on a solution, on Sally.

"When we track down the current host, then we may have a chance of stopping it before it finds Sally again," said Enid.

Enid raised her eyebrows. "Perhaps our new friend Mr Knowles—"

"Alfred," interjected Agnes.

"Perhaps he will find us a witness." She tapped her walking stick and hummed. "I'll ask him to check with his son about any missing persons reports in the past few weeks."

Footsteps approached on the footpath. The female ambulance officer met them.

"Her oxygen levels have improved now." She ushered Enid and

Agnes back to Sally waiting in the ambulance. "There's a nasty burn on her chest."

Enid and Agnes eyed each other. Enid pulled down her long sleeves to cover her forearm.

"The bandages will need changing regularly, but she is refusing to go to Hospital. She needs to be watched for a few days."

"I'll watch her," said Enid.

Water hoses slapped the concrete. Something exploded inside the house. Roof tiles flew into the air and smashed down onto the concrete driveway. Flames leapt above the roof and smoke trickled down the driveway.

A loud roar reverberated around them.

Enid took Sally's hand in hers. "It's all settled, Sally. No arguments: you're coming home with me."

Bacon sizzled in the iron pan, filling the kitchen with a mouth-watering aroma. Enid juggled two fresh eggs in her free hand, pushed the bacon aside with her spatula and cracked the eggs on the side of the pan. Their contents plopped into the pan and sizzled in the oil. She swirled the pan and wriggled the bacon away from the expanding egg whites.

An earthy smell wafted from a second frying pan - warm, rich and velvety. Enid smacked her lips. The mushrooms were almost cooked.

Mr B streaked across the room and wound his body around Enid's legs; his purr seeped into her bones and drowned out the crackle of the bacon.

"Wait your turn, Mr B." Enid stroked his back, wiped her fingers with a hand towel and turned on the coffee machine.

Footsteps thudded softly on the carpet runner along the hall. Sally stood bleary-eyed in the kitchen doorway. Her hair hung in lank tendrils around her face, water dripping onto her shoulders. She rubbed the tips of her hair with a damp towel.

"Good morning, Sally," Enid smiled cheerfully and eyed the growing damp patches on the embroidered cotton dressing gown. "I'm glad I had a spare dressing gown to fit you."

Sally sniffed her hair and coughed. "It still smells of smoke." She stifled another cough and took a deep breath. "Why didn't you wake me?"

"I thought I'd let you sleep in, after yesterday's ordeal."

Sally peered into the kitchen and rubbed her eyes. "Why did you cover the mirror again?"

Enid bit her lip. She didn't like lying to her own flesh and blood. But she had promised Agnes not to tell Sally everything as yet... and omissions weren't technically a lie; a grain of truth was always the best solution.

"Old superstitions die hard I'm afraid." She turned to face Sally. "Mother used to cover the mirrors when someone died."

"I didn't die last night." Sally sucked in a deep breath and stifled another cough. Her breathing was still ragged. "Though... my lungs... disagree." She fumbled in the dressing gown pocket and pulled out an inhaler.

Sally's nose twitched. She sniffed the air. "Oh, Aunt Enid, you shouldn't have gone to all that trouble."

"No trouble at all." Enid lifted the crisped edges of the eggs and slid them onto a clean plate. "Mother always swore a full English breakfast would cure anything."

"I thought a cup of tea was supposed to cure anything?"

"That too, dear. There's a fresh pot on the table." Enid flipped the sausages and bacon onto the plate next to the eggs and shovelled a good dollop of mushrooms over them.

"No, really." Sally's skin paled. She grimaced and covered her mouth. "The meds they gave me have made me nauseated." She closed her eyes and sagged into the closest chair. "I could possibly face some toast."

"Oh, dear, I'm sorry." Enid poured the remaining food onto the plate and placed it on the back of the stovetop to keep warm. "It will keep. I can reheat it for your lunch, if you are feeling better before Agnes picks me up. We have some errands to run."

"You mean snooping?"

"I prefer the term *sleuthing*, dear."

Two pieces of toast jumped out of the toaster.

"There's jam and lemon butter on the table." Enid handed a plate of toast to Sally.

"Thank you, Aunt Enid. What would I do without you?" She curled her feet up onto the chair, teacup in both hands, and sipped her tea.

Enid frowned. She watched Sally's sluggish movements - slow and measured - as she shifted in the chair, stretched her neck and flinched. Her eyes had lost their sparkle; the pain medication had blurred her edges. If only she hadn't dragged Sally into her world...

Enid twisted the hand towel between her fingers. It was too late now. There was no time for recriminations, nor regrets.

She poured herself a cup of coffee, blew on the liquid and took a tentative sip.

The bandage on Sally's chest peeked out from under the neck of her blouse.

"Do you have enough clean bandages?" asked Enid.

Sally sucked on the inhaler and nodded.

"The doctor said it needed changing every day," said Enid.

"I know." Sally shoved the inhaler back into her pocket. "Stop fussing, Aunt Enid." Her feet dropped from the chair. She straightened her shoulders slowly, dug her knife into the jam and slathered it onto her toast. "I'll be fine."

"If I hadn't arrived..." Enid could feel a furrow deepening in her forehead. She wiped her forehead with the hand towel.

Sally's mouth lifted in a weak smile. "But you did," she whispered. "You always do."

Mr B meowed and trotted over to Sally's chair and leapt into her lap. Sally scratched his chin.

"But you can't keep protecting me like I'm still a child." Sally nibbled the corner of her toast and eyed Enid. "When were you going to tell me?"

Enid gulped down her coffee. It scorched all the way down her oesophagus. "Tell you what, dear?"

"What the police said," replied Sally.

"Said about what?" Enid held her breath.

"Your friend, Mrs Oldham. They aren't investigating her death, are they?"

Enid cleared her throat and shook her head. "They say it was natural causes - a heart attack."

"Oh, bollocks!" said Sally.

"Pardon?" Enid raised an eyebrow. There was Sally's spark. It was faint, but it was there.

"Bollocks. That's what you say, isn't it?"

Enid nodded. "And why do you say that?"

"It wasn't a heart attack. I've seen enough of them in the Emergency Department; I don't need to be a doctor to tell you it wasn't a heart attack. Her skin was beet red, not pale or mottled, and there was no cyanosis."

"No what?"

"Cyanosis. It's a bluish tinge around eyes, nose, fingertips. And those burn marks on her chest... It was like she was electrocuted or something." Sally sank her teeth into her toast.

"Surely, the police medical officer would have noticed if there was something strange?" Enid drank the rest of her coffee. She hadn't realised Sally had seen the marks on Olive's chest. Best not draw attention to them; she had promised Agnes. She must not discuss it with Sally. Enid folded the hand towel neatly on the kitchen bench and shuffled towards the back door.

"Where are you off to?" asked Sally.

"To tell the bees you're back."

chapter seven

nid hummed in time with her slippers as they flapped on the concrete pavers in the back yard. The grass tickled her calves.

The screen door rattled and clapped shut under the veranda.

"The grass needs mowing." Sally leaned against the sandstone wall of the house.

Enid nodded and waved her hand in the air. "The new gardener is coming on Saturday."

"The one we saw at the cemetery? Mrs Oldham's grandson?" asked Sally.

"Hmmm."

"You wouldn't be snooping again, would you, Auntie dear?" Sally crunched her toast loudly. "Because the police won't investigate?"

Enid's slippers slapped faster. She hummed louder as she approached the clutch of beehives, pretending to ignore Sally's comment.

"It wouldn't have anything to do with those marks, would it?" asked Sally.

Enid didn't answer.

A warm breeze tickled her face. There was a hint of moisture. She searched the sky: dark clouds gathered above the tree line.

"Hello, darlings," Enid took a key from her pocket, bent down and knocked gently on the hive. "It looks like it's going to rain."

The box vibrated.

"What are they saying?" asked Sally.

Enid straightened up. "That they like you," she replied.

"Really?" Sally raised an eyebrow. "They told you that?"

Enid nodded.

Two bees crawled out of the entrance and onto the top of the box. One lifted off and circled Enid.

"Our Sally has returned," whispered Enid. "She will be staying with us for a while, to recuperate."

A buzz filled the air.

"There's no more news about Olive, I'm afraid."

The wind picked up. It was getting warmer. A single drop of rain splashed onto Enid's cheek.

The bee's buzz lowered in pitch and she drifted back down to the top of the hive to join her companion. They circled each other and vibrated their wings, as if waiting for something to happen.

A third bee flew onto the top of the hive. They wove an intricate dance around each other. Finally, the newcomer rose into the air, hovered, then returned to the hive.

A low murmur grew louder. The box buzzed.

"You did that when I came to house sit, too," said Sally. The toast hovered in front of her mouth. "And when Mrs Oldham died." She pushed herself away from the back wall. "Why do you talk to them?"

Enid turned to Sally and bit her lip again; she couldn't lie to Sally. But if she didn't give the girl something, she would keep questioning.

"It's an old wives' tale where I come from. Though I'm not an old wife, I think I'm old enough for it to count. I tell them all the important news, events like births..." Enid plunged her hands into the pockets of her dressing gown. "Or deaths. Who's coming or going. If you don't they will stop making honey, or leave, or worse - die."

"Die?" Sally stepped forward and halted at the edge of the grass. "Bees could die just because you don't tell them you've had a visitor?" She crunched her toast again.

"They're quite sensitive creatures. Some even believe they are a link between our world and the Other."

The bees' drone crescendoed as if in reply.

"They seem to agree with you."

The buzzing stopped.

Enid spun on her heel to face the hive and placed her ear against the hive box. Not a sound. Not so much as a murmur. Her gaze darted across the sky. The clouds had blackened and rolled closer while she had been distracted. Faint crackles of electricity sparked between them.

Enid's heart plunged into her stomach, knocking the breath from her lungs. She sucked in a sharp breath.

"It's time to go inside, Sally." Enid strained to keep her voice calm.

"It's just a little storm."

Enid searched the bush beyond the back fence. There was no sound, no movement: no bees, no birds twittering, no wind in the trees. Nothing. She scanned the sky as she slapped back along the path towards the house and shooed Sally back inside.

"Please, Sally."

Sally shrugged and entered the cottage.

"And check the kettle, dear. I think we need some tea." Enid waited until Sally's footsteps had faded down the hall, before she closed the screen door and turned to face the back yard.

The clouds continued to sweep across the sky. All *seemed* normal. Enid relaxed. Perhaps it was just a storm?

The clouds stirred.

Enid caught her breath, strode out into the yard, thrust out her hand instinctively - this time without her walking stick to help.

Blast and damnation.

She raised her other arm and swept out in a broad gesture over the yard.

"*Suscita!* Wake up!"

A collective thump echoed over the yard. One. Two. The grass shivered around Enid's feet.

A faint rumble filled the air. The wind swirled, catching the edges of the clouds. Pinpoints of sunlight peeked through the chinks in the darkness. The clouds twisted and retreated back over the hills.

There was a murmur from inside the beehive.

Enid patted the top of the hive. "Thank you, my darlings," she whispered.

The Wolseley coasted along the street to Olive's house. Heat beat down onto the 'mock leather' dashboard and radiated through the car. The afternoon sun glared off the wing mirror and flashed into Enid's eyes. She fanned herself and adjusted the mirror to redirect the glare.

Birds flitted between the trees lining the verge. The Postie's motorcycle puttered along the footpath, darting in and out of driveways as she delivered the mail. The drone of a nearby lawn mower blew in the open passenger side window, bringing with it the delicious smell of freshly cut grass. There seemed no outward sign of Olive's passing.

Enid closed her eyes and took a deep breath. Nothing had changed. Her heart sank. If only they'd known she had been there or known the sacrifice she had made. For them.

Now it was her turn to be there, for Olive's bees. They would be so lonely without Olive to chat to them every day. Enid hadn't checked on them since the funeral - over a week ago. She pursed her lips. Too long. Olive would be livid.

Enid patted the bag on her lap, hoping she'd packed everything they'd need.

"There's Alfred." Agnes' voice was chirpy. "He's keen. Looks like he's already door-knocked most of the street." She nudged Enid with her elbow. "And I don't think that's all he's keen on."

Enid groaned. "Oh, do give up, Agnes. He just a mystery buff, excited to do some real-life sleuthing."

Agnes leaned out of the driver's side window. "Good afternoon, Mr Knowles."

Alfred jotted something in his notebook, tipped his hat in their direction and trotted up the path of the house across the street. Agnes waved back enthusiastically. The car drifted toward the kerb.

Enid grabbed the steering wheel. "Pay attention, Agnes!"

Agnes placed her hand back on the steering wheel. "Hands at ten o'clock and two o'clock. Yes?"

Enid narrowed her eyelids. "You *do* remember, then?"

Agnes harrumphed, steered the car over to the curb and parked in front of Olive's house.

The front gate still hung at a precarious angle. Enid slipped past the orderly perimeter line of garden gnomes along the front fence. Some lay smashed, making the line less orderly.

"Oh, dear," whispered Agnes. "Someone's been here."

"I can see that." Enid tightened her grip on her walking stick. The heady perfume of summer roses engulfed her as she strode up the path to the front door and paused at the hydrangea bushes at the bottom of the front steps; their yellow-tipped leaves were a sickly brown.

Agnes peeked over her shoulder. "Why would someone want to poison Olive's hydrangeas?"

Enid picked a leaf off the nearest bush and rolled it in her fingers. It crunched and crumbled in her hand, as if all the moisture had been drained from it.

"That's not good," she said.

Agnes grabbed a handful of fallen petals and examined them. "They're not blue." She looked at Enid and frowned. "Why are they not blue? Olive knows—" She cleared her throat. "Olive knew better than that. Perhaps that's why she engaged a gardener?" asked Agnes. "To make them blue again?"

Enid dusted off her hand. Agnes wasn't always the sharpest knife in the drawer. But she was loyal.

Enid glanced at the porch. The regimented line of garden gnomes around the house was less bedraggled than that around the fence line, but bedraggled none the less. One of their number lay smashed at the bottom of the front step, hidden under the hydrangea bush.

"Oh, not dear Spike as well?" Enid sifted through the ceramic shards, picked one up and turned it over in her hand. The edges were sooty. She wrapped it in a tissue and slipped it into her bag, then climbed the steps.

Two undamaged garden gnomes guarded the front door. Enid retrieved one of the door gnomes and flipped it over. A plain key was taped to its base.

"Seems whoever it was didn't find what they came for."

Shadows danced across the backyard as the plum tree swayed in the warm wind, its branches scraping the back fence. It was eerily quiet. Only the leaves hissed above her.

Enid scanned the yard. The hose was neatly coiled under the outside water tap. A small garden shed stood near the lemon tree near the side fence. Its missing padlock lay broken on the ground near the door. Two white painted beehives, still draped with the black crepe ribbon Enid had placed there on day of Olive's funeral, stood next to the garage under the plum tree.

Agnes' footsteps crunched along the gravel of the side driveway behind her. "They've broken into the shed as well?"

Enid nodded. "I just hope the bees are safe."

She walked past the garden shed and paused under the lemon tree. A sharp smell lingered. Agnes joined her under the tree and sniffed the air. She screwed up her nose and jumped out from under the canopy.

"What on earth, Agnes!"

"Smells like her Simon has fertilised the tree recently. I don't relish cleaning chicken manure off my shoes again." Agnes limped back to the concrete path and checked her shoes.

"Do stop fussing. You'll scare the bees." Enid glanced at the hives, hummed a calming tune, and examined the ground at her feet. A few scattered lemons peppered the un-worked soil. "Agnes, there's nothing. Olive hasn't—" Enid sniffed the air and continued to hum. There was a definite smell of nitrate. She knew that smell. The last note of the tune faltered. Her gaze darted over the back yard and settled on the beehives in the far corner. She swallowed and tentatively hummed a new tune, this time to calm herself.

A breeze caught the end of a black crepe ribbon and tapped it against the silent hive.

Silent?

Enid's heart jumped into her throat. She swallowed, stepped back under the lemon tree's protective canopy and scanned the sky, trying to calm her rapid breaths.

"What's wrong?" Agnes slipped her foot back into her shoe.

"The bees," replied Enid. "They're too quiet." She raised her walking stick, held it like a sword ready to strike, and scanned the sky again. The sun blazed down, casting sharp-edged shadows across the yard; there wasn't a cloud in the sky.

Agnes cringed and retreated back under the tree with Enid.

"Can you see anything?" she asked.

Enid shook her head and took a step forward.

Agnes grabbed Enid's arm. "It may not be safe."

"We'll soon find out." Enid stepped into the sunlight, raised her eyes to the sky and waited.

"But the bees are never wrong, Enid," whispered Agnes.

"No, they're not." Enid spoke slowly as the tip of her walking stick fell to the ground. A horrid thought had formed in her mind. Her carpetbag slipped from her hand. Her knees wobbled, as if all her years had descended upon her at once. She leaned her weight on her walking stick to keep her balance and staggered toward the hives. Agnes hobbled behind her still fussing with her shoe.

Remnants of biscuits were scattered across the ground beside the hive. A toppled glass of wine had left red stains spattered on its white painted wood - all that was left of the food from Olive's wake.

Enid strained to hear any noise - a faint buzz, a scratching of movement. Anything. There was nothing. The hives were as silent as a tomb.

She took a deep breath and hummed a few tentative notes. Usually bees would be crawling over the hive, buzzing around her in welcome, or flying in and out of the entry hole or landing platform at the bottom of the hive. But there was no movement.

Enid tapped the wood gently. Not one bee crawled out to investigate.

"Enid, are they—?"

Enid didn't reply. The air smelled of burnt wax. She held her breath as she checked the entry hole. A thin line of wax sealed the lower entrance. She touched the wood of the landing platform. Fine grains of wax and dirt stuck to her finger.

"No." The words barely left her lips as she exhaled and tried to catch her breath.

Agnes hurried across the yard, Enid's bag cradled in her arms. "Have they swarmed?" she asked. "I thought you'd told them? Why did they—?"

"Oh, do stop prattling, Agnes," hissed Enid. "They didn't swarm." She grabbed her bag, extracted a hive tool and gently pried the lid away from the top storage box and leaned it against the hive "Can't you smell that?"

The smell of burnt wax was stronger now. But there was more - a strong smell of wood smoke. Enid examined the combs. Most of the wooden frames were blackened, almost charcoaled in places. Her hands shook as she slipped the end of the tool between the scorched combs. Chunks crumbled from the edge and rattled to the bottom of the box.

Agnes stared in horror at the hive.

Enid shifted the comb sideways to loosen the wax, handed the tool to Agnes and gently lifted the comb out of the box. Patches of singed, inanimate bees lined the frame and crowded around soot-filled food and pollen cells.

She removed the top box and pried apart the combs, this time from the middle of the brood box of the hive. They felt heavier than the previous combs. Perhaps there was some hope?

Enid leaned closer. There was a faint buzz in the centre of the hive. Her heart skipped. She lifted the frame and scrutinised the comb looking for any sign of movement.

There!

She gripped the frame and turned it toward the sunlight. A cluster of bees danced groggily around a small patch of undamaged larvae cells. She scanned them for any sign of the queen bee, with a longer body and larger—. Enid's shoulders slumped. The queen's wings were singed. Drones crawled around her foraging for traces of pollen in the comb cells.

"I'm so sorry," whispered Enid. Her jaw clenched. "I should have come earlier."

Enid pulled a small eyedropper bottle from her bag. A sweet smell rose from the liquid in the opened bottle. If she could nurse the queen back to health she could find the hive a new home. A safe home.

Agnes tugged on her blouse. "Ask them what happened."

Enid wiped a tear from her eye and hummed a gentle tune.

Enid slipped the door key into the back door.

"Did you see the footprints?" asked Enid.

Agnes squinted at the depression in the soil near the back door.

"About size twelve, I'd guess."

"Good guess." Enid nodded. "And they've been disturbed." Enid turned the key in the lock. "Something has been dragged or rolled over them."

Agnes continued to examine the marks. "But there's no other footprints," she said.

"I know."

The door opened with a click.

Agnes circled the footprints and peered back along their progress, from the beehives.

"What did the bees say?" The screen door rattled as Agnes slipped past Enid.

"Olive's grandson was here that afternoon; they didn't like the noise of the mower. Otherwise they heard nothing - not until it was too late. There was something glowing in a dark cloud, then blackness and scorching heat." Enid closed her eyes; the image of glowing red eyes had burned into her memory. "They had no chance of escape."

"Perhaps The Collector attacked her?" asked Agnes.

Enid opened her eyes. "Or it was the host?"

"Is this where you found her?" Agnes stood at the end of the island bench, staring at the floor.

"Yes."

Enid entered the kitchen. The fruit had been replaced in the fruit bowl and had already wrinkled in the heat. The broken jars of lemon butter had been cleaned up and the remaining jars stacked neatly in the open pantry.

Agnes picked something up from the floor and examined it. "You missed a bit," she said.

"I had other things on my mind," replied Enid.

Agnes placed the remnant on the island bench. It was a piece of clear glass, crusted with dried lemon butter. A few ants scurried across the marble bench top.

Enid noticed a black smudge on the back of Agnes' blouse as she turned to check the pantry.

"You've got soot all over you." Enid turned Agnes to face the sink and brushed her fingers over the material.

"Pardon?"

Enid rubbed the substance between her fingers. It was oily, with a faint smell of... urea? She thrust her smudged fingers under Agnes' nostrils.

"Agnes, where have you been?"

Agnes screwed up her nose. "Where did that come from?"

"That's what I'd like to know." Enid sniffed the oily soot again. "It smells like the scorch marks in the hive."

They traced Agnes' footsteps onto the back veranda. The screen door flapped shut.

"There it is again." Enid sniffed the air and stared at the screen door. She ran her finger down the fly screen and examined the black fingertips. It was the same oily residue on Agnes' blouse, the scorched frames of the hive combs and on poor Spike, the garden gnome.

"The Collector?" whispered Agnes.

"It must leave a mark where it enters and—" Enid rushed over to the sink window and sniffed. She wiped a clean finger along the fly screen mesh, checked the tip. "And where it leaves."

Enid sucked in a sharp breath and scowled. "I should have realised."

"Realised what?" asked Agnes.

"I've seen this once before." Enid tapped her walking stick and cursed her faltering memory under her breath. What else had she forgotten? "It was before you joined us. The last time The Dark almost broke through..." Enid swallowed. "When your predecessor died. Just before you were—"

"Recruited." Agnes crossed her arms.

Enid removed a handkerchief from her bag and wiped the soot from her fingers, avoiding Agnes' stare. "I wish Olive was here. She had more experience than me. The incident was almost all over by the time I arrived."

"Surely Olive would have recorded it in *The Books*?"

Enid shoved the handkerchief back in her bag and snapped it shut. "Of course, *The Books*!"

Olive kept a journal. They all did. Even young Agnes. Olive was the oldest of them, having been a Protector long before her family emigrated to Australia; she would have an entire library of information by now.

"What a fool I am!" hissed Enid. She had been distracted by Sally's attack and forgotten the first rule of engagement: know your enemy. They needed *The Books*. She would not make the same mistake again.

The gravel crunched along the side of the house.

Agnes flinched. "It's back!"

"No, dear. A Collector wouldn't just trot up the drive in broad daylight." Enid gripped her walking stick; she wasn't about to be caught off-guard again.

The screen door rattled. They turned to see Alfred hurry in through the back door. His cheeks were flushed, his nose bright red.

"Good afternoon, Alfred." Agnes' voice lifted an octave.

"Mission accomplished." He puffed and fanned himself with his hat. "I see the hooligans have already taken pot shots at the garden ornaments." He shuffled across the kitchen and leaned on the island bench. "How on earth did you manage to get inside? They didn't break through the back door as well?"

"I have many secrets, Alfred," said Enid.

Alfred's cheeks reddened even more. He peered at the back door lock and raised an eyebrow. "Did you pick the lock?" He grinned. "You'll have to teach me."

"I used the key," Enid replied flatly.

Alfred's eyebrow dropped.

"Are you all right, Alfred?" asked Agnes. "Sit down. You look like you will pass out."

"That will happen when you wear a three-piece suit in the middle of summer," said Enid.

"It's my sleuthing suit," said Alfred, "like Poirot." He opened his jacket to reveal a patchwork of hidden pockets with pencils, notebooks, a Swiss army knife and a set of lock picks. "You never know what you'll need when on a case."

Enid raised an eyebrow. "Does your son know you carry that around? You could be arrested for 'intent'."

"Not if I can't use them."

"Are you sure about that?" said Enid.

Alfred's smile flickered. He straightened his shoulders and buttoned his jacket.

Agnes glared at Enid. "Any luck with the door knock?" she asked Alfred.

His eyes lit up. "Yes." He pulled a small notebook from a pocket and flipped it open.

"Did anyone see a blue trailer?" asked Enid.

"Yes, the gardener's." Alfred's notebook drooped. "How did you know?"

"Some friends told me, but they weren't sure of the time."

"I can help with that." He read out his notes. "Mrs Luske, across the road at number fifteen, confirmed there was a dark blue utility truck and trailer parked outside for most of the afternoon of—"

"The accident?" ventured Agnes.

"Yes." Alfred cleared his throat. "She said it belonged to Mrs

Oldham's grandson, though she didn't see him at all."

"That would be Simon," said Enid.

"It's possible he saw something," said Agnes.

"I'll ask him on Saturday when he comes over to look at the garden," replied Enid. "I'm sure he'd love some scones and jam. Or perhaps chocolate cake?"

"You always get to do the asking." Agnes tapped her foot on the tiles.

"I have seniority," she whispered and turned back to face Alfred. "Anything else, Alfred?"

"Yes." Alfred continued to read from the notebook: "The vehicle left before sunset and has returned twice over the past week. It was last here yesterday." He closed the notebook. "She assumed he was here clearing out the estate."

"Oh, I hadn't thought of that."

"Thought of what?" asked Agnes.

Enid leaned close to Agnes and whispered: "What if Simon found *The Books* and thought they were just old diaries?"

"And threw them away?" Agnes' eyes widened.

"Or if The Collector found them?" Enid's heart froze. "We need to find them."

Alfred cleared his throat. "Can I assist you, ladies?"

Agnes went quiet. Enid bit her lip. If she couldn't tell Sally - her own flesh and blood - how could she tell Alfred - a civilian, and relative stranger?

Olive was the only one of them to have experienced The Dark's Final Collections first hand, they needed her notes, her knowledge. If they were to have any chance of discovering The Dark's weakness, they needed her *Books*. And they *needed* them now - *before* The Collector found them.

Agnes frowned and grabbed Enid's arm. "No, Enid. We agreed not to—"

Trust me, Enid mouthed in reply.

Enid turned to face Alfred. "We need to find Olive's diaries."

"Righty-O, I'm on it." He slipped his notebook back into his coat pocket and strode toward the hallway door.

"You can't," Agnes whispered.

Enid held up her hand to silence Agnes. "And, Alfred," said Enid. "They *are* personal."

He turned and nodded. "I was raised a gentleman. I would never read anyone's personal papers without permission, especially that of a lady."

Agnes' grip on Enid's arm loosened.

"Thank you, Alfred. Olive would appreciate it."

Alfred placed his hat back on his head, patted it in place and strode down the hallway.

Books lay scattered over the floor of the lounge room. Several others had been dislodged from bookshelves that lined every available inch of wall space; some dangled precariously from the single shelf running above the top of the front window, bridging the shelves on either side. Even more were scattered over Olive's computer desk in the far corner.

Someone had definitely been rummaging through Olive's library. Enid sighed. Olive would've been horrified to see her 'library' in such a state.

Enid dropped her carpetbag onto the couch and picked up a book from the closest dishevelled pile - a hardcover treatise on Apiculture, wrapped in a full-colour cover boasting a most pleasing rendition of a honey bee returning to its hive. She slipped it into her bag, rescued the entire pile and set them down on the coffee table.

She checked each book in turn - reference books on thermodynamics, various mythology books, scientific papers on the Multiverse and various historical herbal treatises - and returned them to the bookshelves. Olive had always had her nose in some new research in an effort to keep up with the world as it changed around them.

Enid scanned the room. There were so many books. It was like the proverbial needle in a haystack. She needed help. She twitched her fingers.

"*Revelare.*"

Her fingertips tingled and crackled as she raised her hand and waved it across the room, warming as they pointed in the direction of the desk. The tingle crept down her fingers to her hand and dug into her palm. Enid flinched and shook the pain from her hand as she picked her way across the room toward the desk.

The desk was a shambles. Books on chess and poker strategy were strewn across the desktop and partially covered Olive's laptop.

Enid tugged at the drawer, expecting it to be locked, and almost slipped off the office chair as the drawer slid open. She grabbed the desk to regain her balance and peered into the drawer. Nothing. Someone had broken the lock and cleared it out already.

"Nothing in the bedroom." Agnes entered the lounge room. "Someone's definitely been in there. Everything's been searched."

"Perhaps it was Simon collecting his grandmother's valuables?"

"No," replied Agnes. "The jewellery is untouched. The bookshelf and linen chest have been raided, though."

"Olive's desk has been broken into as well." Enid spun in her chair and examined the desk. Her chest tightened. "The Collector must know about *The Books.*"

"Perhaps there's a clue on the computer?" asked Agnes.

"How?" Enid screwed up her nose. She didn't own a computer - and there was a reason for it; they hated her. Or she hated them. Perhaps it was a mutual thing?

"You really need to watch more television, Enid. Those modern detectives are always finding clues on social media. Olive loved that computer. Perhaps we could check some of those poker sites? Or chat to one of her chess champion friends?"

Enid cleared away the books, stacked them in a pile, opened the laptop and smiled. Olive played online chess games and relished her regular online poker challenges, as she called them. She was a keen strategist and could outwit any General of The Dark's horde. Enid tapped a few keys. Perhaps there *would* be something on the confounded contraption?

The laptop bleeped.

"It wants a password," said Agnes.

Enid frowned. "How would I know?" she hissed.

"Know what?" Alfred stood in the doorway and wiped beads of perspiration from his forehead.

"The password," replied Agnes.

"I can't get it to work without one. Can I?" asked Enid.

Alfred shook his head. "I could ask Tom to have a look at it. I could say I've forgotten my password. They've got people who specialise in that sort of thing."

"No, thank you, Alfred." Enid closed the laptop and shook her head. "I'm sure Olive wouldn't want strangers peeking at her personal affairs on the Internets, even if it was a police detective."

"Perhaps your Sally could take a look?" Agnes bit her lip, creating a lop-sided smile. "She's good with computers."

"Good idea." Enid tugged at the power cord. "Did you find anything, Alfred?"

"Nothing in the bathroom or the spare bedroom, I'm sorry," he replied.

"*The Books?*" whispered Agnes.

Enid's fingers tangled in the cord, almost dragging the laptop off the desk. She cursed under her breath. Were they too late; had *The Books* been found? Her heart sank. If so, The Collector would learn their secrets. They would have lost any meagre advantage they may have.

Agnes plopped down onto the couch. "What do we do now, Enid?"

"We need another clue," replied Enid. "Alfred, have you had a chance to speak to Tom yet?"

"I see him tomorrow." Alfred smiled and tapped his nose. "I haven't forgotten, Enid. You wanted to know about missing persons, correct?"

Enid nodded. The Dark only needed thirteen souls to gain enough energy to break through fully. They needed to know how close The Dark was to Final Collection. She shoved the laptop into her bag.

"Come over to mine as soon as you find out."

"I'll need your address." Alfred straightened his shoulders.

"You can pick up Agnes on the way. She can tell you where to go."

"Oh." Alfred's shoulders slumped slightly.

Enid collected up the laptop and power cord and bundled them into her bag and strode into the hall. Agnes trailed behind.

Alfred trotted up beside her. "Wait, Enid, I almost forgot."

Enid paused mid-step. "Forgot what?"

"Your cards won at Bingo the other night." Alfred shoved his hand into his pocket and pulled out his wallet.

Enid stayed his hand. "Keep it," she said, "for services rendered."

Alfred blushed.

"She means for your help with the door knock and with your son, Tom," whispered Agnes.

Enid spun on her heel, smiled and marched toward the kitchen.

chapter eight

the hum of the car engine faded along the road. Enid waved goodbye to Agnes, latched the front gate behind her and greeted her beloved garden gnomes.

Gold paint peeled off the nose of the closest ornament.

"Good afternoon, Nugget."

She nodded in the direction of the swing chair.

"All quiet, Red?" Enid paused and scanned the grassed area usually occupied by the scarlet-clad gnome. Tall blades of grass wafted in the warm breeze. There was no sign of Red's shiny scarlet cap. She waved her walking stick over the top of the grass, pushing it aside to search the area more thoroughly.

"Red?" Enid scanned the front yard. All the familiar faces were there: Nugget, Oscar, Frosty and Timble, all standing to attention at their designated sentry posts. She lowered her walking stick.

Red was not there.

Enid trotted into the cottage and discarded her carpetbag onto the hall table.

"Has anyone been in the front yard, Sally?" she asked.

There was no reply.

"Do you feel up to dinner, Sally?" said Enid as she walked down the hall.

Enid wandered into the kitchen and lifted down her apron from the back of the kitchen door. Clean dishes filled the drying rack. Tea towels hung from the side of the wood stove. The curtains tugged in the warm breeze.

There was still no sign of Sally.

Enid tied up her apron as she strolled down the hall toward the lounge room.

The late afternoon sun shone through the front window and bathed Enid's favourite armchair with warm light. Mr B was curled up on its cushion, snoring quietly.

"Where's Sally, Mr B?" she asked.

The cat's ears pricked up. He opened an eye, yawned, and snapped the eyelid closed, without moving an inch.

Enid huffed. "You're no help."

She walked off in the direction of the bedrooms.

Sally's bedspread was neatly tucked into the footboard with tightly folded corners. Her sandshoes were placed neatly under the chair next to the wardrobe, and her uniform hung from the side of the standing mirror's carved frame. Everything was in order; there was no sign of any disturbance.

And still no sign of Sally.

A gully breeze caught Sally's uniform and knocked the clothes hanger against the mirror.

Enid peered out the open window to check the back yard. It was quiet.

"Where are you, girl?"

She crossed the room, sidestepped the mirror and walked behind it to reach the window. She opened the flyscreen and leaned out. The old sun lounge had been dragged from under the veranda onto the grass. A small table had been set up beside it.

The heat beat down onto the dry grass. The gully wind subsided as the North wind picked up. Dust burned Enid's nostrils. She paused near the edge of the veranda.

The sun lounge lay just beyond the shade, its multi-coloured, woven plastic back facing the cottage. Its back sagged generously from all the years of supporting the weight of a lounging body. A ring of garden gnomes surrounded it. The distinctive silhouette of Red's cap peeked out from the grass at the head of the sun lounge, on the opposite side to the table: fine silver cracks traced his scarlet cap, converging on a small white chink near the tip - the remaining scar from his previous adventure - where the final sliver was never found.

The back of the sun lounge shivered. A bright pink hand, holding a glass of iced tea, snaked away from behind its cover. The glass rattled as it was placed onto the table.

Bees buzzed lazily in the air, drifted closer and greeted Enid. She smiled and nodded.

"Sally, I'm back."

The sun lounge wobbled. Two sunburnt legs swung onto the grass and nudged the gnomes closest to the chair. Red's cap teetered. Enid flinched. The cap steadied and remained standing.

Sally turned to face Enid; her bright pink nose poked out from under an over-sized green sun hat.

"Oh, hello, Aunt Enid."

"Are you feeling better, dear? I was just about to start dinner," replied Enid.

Sally lowered the book in her hand and glanced at her mobile phone on the table. "Is that the time already?"

A bee circled Sally's head. She ducked as it sped toward Enid.

"Did you enjoy your sleuthing trip?" Sally's smile puffed up her cheeks, making them appear like ripe tomatoes.

"Oh, dear." Enid touched her nose. "I think you've gotten a bit too much sun. You should know better, with your fair skin."

Sally removed her hat, prodded her cheeks, and winced.

Enid glanced down at Sally's bare feet. "And look at your toes!"

Sally wiggled her toes and frowned.

"I did have a hat and sunscreen. I just lost track of time. I was chatting to your bees." The book slapped shut in her hand. "Though the conversation was a little one-sided."

Another bee buzzed near Enid's ear. "So I hear." She glanced at the green-bound journal in Sally's hand and nodded.

"It must be a good book," said Enid.

Sally slipped the journal behind her back.

The air stilled. Enid peered at the gum trees. They were silent, except for the rustle of the leaves as a faint, hot wind rushed up the gully. She scanned the back yard. The roving worker bees were no longer there. They had abandoned the yard and flown back to the hive.

Enid cocked her head to listen. The hive had stopped talking.

Her heart raced as she scanned the sky for any sign of a Collector.

Nothing. She took a deep breath. Still, one couldn't be too careful.

"Sally, come inside the house. It's not safe." She beckoned Sally toward the veranda.

"I know, Aunt Enid." Sally stood, straightened her denim shorts and stretched each of her limbs tentatively. "I'm a nurse; I should know better, but it's after five-twenty. The U.V. level would've dropped by now."

Enid stepped closer to the edge of the veranda and eyed the darkening sky.

"Inside, girl." Enid huffed and nudged Sally toward the door.

"All right." Sally snatched up her iced tea. Remnants of ice jiggled and tinkled against the glass. "But I'm not a child any more. I'd like to have some answers."

The screen door slammed behind her as she disappeared into the shadows of the hall.

Enid held her breath and watched the dark clouds as they twisted in the sky and seemed to retreat - just a little.

Sally nestled into the padded armchair near the front lounge room window. She watched Mr B as he traced the perimeter of the room, marking his territory as he rubbed his body on each bookshelf in turn. He paused near a book, sniffed and meowed. Sally glanced at the shelf. A treatise on beekeeping had been wedged amongst the permaculture gardening books. She winced; it had taken her most of the holiday to re-order her aunt's shelves in alphabetical order - and a mere week for Aunt Enid to muddle it up again. How could her aunt ever find *anything*?

Sally climbed out of the armchair and re-filed the book. She glanced along the shelves and sighed. She'd read almost every one of the books: classics, 'how to' books, recipe books. Aunt Enid needed to invest in some fresh reading material.

Sally picked up the green journal and slouched back into the armchair. But this was new. She'd found it hidden inside a hollowed out hardcover book. Very curious. It was a hand-written manuscript, full of action and adventure. A rollicking fantasy story, spanning generations. Each page was dated - like a diary.

Sally opened the book to the last page she'd read and removed the ribbon bookmark. The handwriting was sometimes scribbled, but was definitely her aunt's; she recognised it from the family recipe books in the kitchen. It was dated: *Monday, 27th September, 1920.* She was barely one-third through...

Sally turned the page eagerly. She hadn't picked Aunt Enid as a writer; this was a good yarn, so why hide it?

Mr B circled the chair, rubbed his entire body along Sally's foot. He blinked his deep blue eyes and purred. She leaned down and scratched his chin.

"Oh, all right, but don't get too comfortable." She patted her lap.

Aunt Enid blustered into the lounge room and made a beeline for the front window. She stared out as she fussed with the curtains.

Sally lowered the manuscript and concealed it on her lap, behind Mr B.

"Are you all right, Aunt Enid?"

"Oh... um..." Aunt Enid straightened the curtains. "I can't find my... walking stick."

"Why would it be in the front yard?" Sally frowned. It wasn't like Aunt Enid to misplace things. "It's in the umbrella stand, in the hall."

Aunt Enid glanced out of the window, seemingly distracted. Sally fingered the manuscript. The story was full of strange portents and attacks from the heavens... Sally's heart sank. Perhaps her aunt was taking it all too seriously, like in her book? There was Uncle Edward after all...

Sally slipped the bookmark into the pages and repositioned the journal so Aunt Enid couldn't see it from where she stood. Best not to aggravate her further.

Aunt Enid turned slowly, craned her neck as if to spy what was hidden in Sally's lap and clicked her tongue.

"Go, make yourself useful, Mr B. Catch some mice or something." Aunt Enid shooed him away.

Mr B stretched and stepped off Sally's lap, as if levitating down to the floor.

Aunt Enid stared at the journal in Sally's lap, and raised an eyebrow. Heat crept up Sally's neck.

Aunt Enid held out her hand. Sally cringed; there was nowhere to hide. It was like being back at school, the teacher reprimanding her for passing notes.

"That's private," said Enid.

"I'm sorry." Sally relinquished the journal to her aunt.

"How much did you read?"

"It's very good," whispered Sally.

Aunt Enid glared at her.

"Really, it *is*."

Her aunt's glare softened. "Pardon?" She snatched the journal and slipped it into her apron pocket.

"Your book," replied Sally. "Why didn't you tell me you were writing a novel? And a fantasy; all that work - that's impressive."

"It's just an old woman's ramblings," said Aunt Enid.

"Nonsense. Some of the best fantasy writers are..." Sally paused. "have experience. You're in great company: Ursula le Guin, for example."

Sally glanced over her aunt's bookshelves. This was the perfect chance to encourage her aunt to widen the range of her reading material.

"You've probably read these a thousand times. I'll buy you some of her books. I think you'd enjoy them."

Aunt Enid gripped her apron pocket and didn't reply.

"Don't worry, I won't tell *The Marple Brigade*."

"The what?" asked Aunt Enid with a quizzical look.

"Aunt Agnes and Mr Knowles - your sleuthing buddies. It will be our secret."

Her aunt relaxed her grip on the apron.

Crisis averted. Sally leaned back in the armchair. The bandage on her chest tugged the skin, irritating her injury. She scratched at the dressing and winced.

Aunt Enid's shoulders tensed.

Sally shifted in the armchair to relieve the discomfort of the bandage - and that of a nagging question: Why was her thermal burn the same as Olive Oldham's scar? Her aunt hadn't realised she'd seen it. Sally straightened her shoulders; now was as good a time as any to get some answers.

"But you must tell me one thing." Sally narrowed her eyelids. "Tell me about Mrs Oldham's scar."

Aunt Enid sucked in a breath and glanced over Sally's shoulder, past the drifting curtain. "What scar, dear?"

Sally stood by her aunt's shoulder. What was so engaging in the front yard? She glanced out the window. There was nothing there. Her stomach knotted. She loved her great aunt dearly, but she seemed to be more distracted of late - more obsessed with the weather, for one thing.

The storm clouds hung low in the sky.

"Aunt Enid?" Sally placed her hand gently on her aunt's shoulder.

Aunt Enid's gaze snapped back toward her. Sally stared into her aunt's eyes. The sparkle was still there - sharp as ever. The knots in her stomach began to untie. Aunt Enid wasn't losing it yet.

However... there were extra lines framing her aunt's eyes. She was worried about something. But what?

Sally puffed out her cheeks. "You don't need to keep secrets from me."

Silence.

"I'm thirty-one. I'm not the child who used to visit you in the holidays, anymore. I've seen things that would make your hair curl, like some of the old biddies at bingo night."

Aunt Enid's voice was measured. "Is that so?"

Sally wasn't going to let it go. She had seen the scar on Mrs Oldham's shoulder - the same as the burn on her own chest. She *needed* answers.

"I changed my dressing today." Sally pulled down her top and peeled the bandage away from her skin to reveal the angry burn. "The burn - caused by the necklace you gave me; it's the same as hers."

Aunt Enid's eyes widened. She twisted away from Sally's hand. "I didn't know that would happen."

"I don't blame you, Aunt Enid."

Aunt Enid's shoulders relaxed.

Sally delved into a pocket of her denim shorts and pulled out the necklace her aunt had given to her. She held the chain and let the pendant dangle. The blue stone glinted in the late afternoon light.

Her aunt's face went pale; she hovered for a moment then circled closer, all attention on Sally and necklace.

"It belonged to her didn't it? Your friend?"

Aunt Enid stared at the pendant and swallowed.

Sally flipped the pendant back into her hand. Her aunt's gaze followed its movements as though hypnotised.

"I saw the scar on her shoulder," said Sally. "It was the same shape as my burn." Sally frowned. "Why did you lie to me?"

"I didn't lie, Sally." Aunt Enid seemed entranced by the necklace.

"You said it was a family heirloom, that it was good luck." Sally clenched the necklace in her fist. "It hasn't been so far."

"Sally, you need to put that back on." Her aunt clenched her fingers.

"Not until you tell me what is going on. Tell me. Please." Sally fought back angry tears. She couldn't believe her aunt would willingly deceive her. "Don't you trust me?"

Aunt Enid's gaze flickered back toward the window. "It's not that simple. I—"

A horn honked in the driveway. Sally glanced through the window. A shiny BMW sat in the driveway. A well-dressed gentleman, in a three-piece suit, shut the car door, adjusted a thick, official-looking folder under his arm, and strode toward the front door.

Aunt Enid bustled into the hallway.

Sally shoved the necklace back into her pocket and took a deep breath to prepare herself for the charge of the *Marple Brigade*.

Enid opened the front door; Alfred stood on the porch, his jacket buttoned and a bulging packet under his arm.

"I see you're in uniform," Enid eyed Alfred's 'sleuthing suit'.

"May I come in?" Alfred wiped his shoes on the doormat - out of habit, Enid assumed; it hadn't rained for over a week.

The cat flap slapped at the back door and a patter of feline paws rushed along the hallway toward them.

"To what do I owe the pleasure of your company so soon, Alfred?" Enid stepped to one side, trying not to trip over Mr B as he twisted between her legs and nudged her, as she retreated toward the lounge room.

"I have new clues." Alfred presented Enid with a thick document folder. "Information on all ten of the local missing persons in the past month."

Enid halted near the hall table.

"Ten?" She gasped, as if she'd been punched in the chest, and struggled to breathe, to remain calm. The Dark needed thirteen souls to breach the shell of its Otherworld, in order to enter this world. She reached for her walking stick - partly for protection, partly to stay upright. Her grip tightened on its handle. "That many, already?"

"Already?" asked Alfred.

"I mean..." Enid regained her balance and slowly straightened her back. "I didn't realise there would be so many."

She removed the thick elastic band from the folder and looked inside. It was full of police reports, many misaligned as if photocopied in haste. "My, you are thorough, Alfred. I'm surprised Tom let you copy them."

"He didn't." Alfred scuffed his feet on the carpet. "Well, not exactly. I just happened to be in the vicinity of his office this afternoon, when he was..." He paused. "When he was called away. An anonymous phone call; every lead must be checked, after all." Alfred straightened his jacket. "Father always said: 'Never waste an opportunity'."

"Really?" Enid raised an eyebrow. "I'm impressed at your sneakiness,

Alfred."

Alfred grinned. "Did you know you can load a ream of paper into one end of those photocopy contraptions and just press a button and, whoosh! It automatically copies them all - and keeps them in order for you? Whatever will they think of next?"

His pale blue eyes sparkled in excitement; he was enjoying playing detective - the chase. Enid resisted the urge to laugh. That would be cruel.

"Did you come all the way up the Hill just to give me these?" Enid waved a few papers in the air. "You could've shown me tomorrow at our arranged meeting, when Agnes was here as well."

Alfred's fingers slipped away from the edge of his jacket.

"No, I needed to tell you: Tom received the report about your niece's house fire, from the Metro Fire Service. Something about the door? They think it may have been a planned attack." He removed his hat. "They've started an investigation. It seems there was a connection between Mrs Oldham's death and your niece's attack. I thought you'd like to know as soon as possible."

"They took their time." Enid sighed. Now they weren't the only ones searching for a suspect. Perhaps The Collector's host would be found soon, with the police finally doing their job - though, as far as they knew, the attacker was only human.

"They want to talk to your niece," said Alfred. "About her injuries."

Enid glanced toward the lounge room and stepped away from the door. She spoke in a whisper: "Sally?" Of course they'd want to speak to Sally. Why was she surprised?

Alfred lowered his voice: "They think the same person tried to attack both Mrs Oldham and your niece." He fidgeted with his hat. "And there's similar suspicious incidents with some of the other missing persons. We may have stumbled onto a serial killer, Enid."

Enid's heart raced. How many of them had been taken by The

Collector?

"She will be safe, Enid." Alfred's fingers reached for Enid's arm, and hesitated. "Tom is very good at his job." He patted her arm gently, then snapped his fingers back to the rim of his hat. He cleared his throat. "I was also wondering if you'd found anything on Olive's computer yet?"

"No, I haven't asked Sally to look at it yet." In truth, she'd forgotten about it in all the excitement. She reached for her carpetbag on the hall table.

"Computer?" Sally's voice rolled down the hallway.

Enid glanced back toward the lounge room. Sally leaned against doorframe.

"Did you steal your friend's laptop, Aunt Enid?"

"Borrowed, dear."

"We were hoping there were clues on it," said Alfred.

Sally smiled at Alfred. "What exactly are you looking for?" she asked.

Enid pulled the laptop out of the bag and clutched it to her chest. She needed to know if Olive had left any clues on it. Sally was the only person she could trust to investigate, without divulging too much and risking the further wrath of Agnes. Perhaps if she used the ruse Sally herself had concocted? A novel was not too far from the truth, and should avoid too many more questions...

"Something for a book," replied Enid.

"A book?" Alfred's face lit up.

"Another one?" asked Sally as she ushered Alfred into the lounge room.

"Olive was writing the book with me." Enid bit her lip; she hated deceiving her own niece. "We were writing it together." Not a lie. "I couldn't find her notes. I was hoping she'd saved them on her computer."

"You didn't tell me you were a writer, Enid," said Alfred.

Sally nodded and stepped forward. "She's writing a fantasy mystery.

She didn't even tell me." Sally's lip curled as she took the laptop.

"Mysteries?" He turned to face Enid. "Our very own Christie? Why am I not surprised?" He dropped his hat onto the lounge chair. "Will I be in it?"

Enid stood in the doorway and leaned on her walking stick. So much for avoiding awkward questions.

Sally sidled up next to her and raised an eyebrow. "So this is why you kept looking out the window all afternoon?" she whispered to Enid.

Heat crept up Enid's neck and across her cheeks.

"You didn't tell me you had a boyfriend, Aunt Enid."

Enid flinched. "He's not my—"

Sally took the laptop, grinned and spun on her heel to face Alfred. "Pleased to meet you, Mr...?"

"Mr Knowles," replied Enid. "Alfred, this is my great niece, Sally Hunter."

Alfred inclined his head in a quick bow. "Likewise, Miss Hunter."

"Sally," said Sally with a smile, as she wandered into the lounge room and opened the laptop on the coffee table.

Mr B curled his tail around Enid's calf as she eyed the pair; they chatted, like old friends oblivious to her presence.

"I'll make a cuppa then." Enid strode into the kitchen, Mr B padding silently behind her.

chapter nine

C hina cups rattled on the tea tray.

"I thought you might like some scones, Alfred," said Enid.

"Excellent." Alfred clapped his hands and sat on one end of the lounge chair next to his hat. He glanced up at Enid, lifted his hat and smiled.

"There's fresh tea in the pot." Enid put the tray on the coffee table and sat in the armchair opposite him.

Alfred's smile sagged, as he replaced his hat on the lounge.

Mr B slinked into the room and stood at attention by Enid's foot. His tail twitched as he watched Alfred's every move.

"I'm in." Sally leaned back from Olive's laptop and poured herself a cup of tea.

"The password was 'Sylvia'," whispered Alfred. "I don't know how she guessed it so quickly."

"I must've read it somewhere," said Sally as she tapped the keyboard.

"I wonder where?" Enid untied her apron, clutched '*The Book*' in the pocket and tucked it next to the padded cushion of her chair.

"There's a lot of on-line poker and chess games." Sally ignored her aunt's grumbles. "And a word file." She turned the screen to face Aunt Enid and pointed to a file named: *The Book*.

Enid shifted in her chair and gritted her teeth. Olive couldn't have made it more obvious! At least Sally thought it was just a story - a fantasy. And, so far, Alfred believed the ruse too. Just as well Agnes wasn't here to scold her.

"It looks like the manuscript you're looking for," continued Sally. "There were a few more passwords needed to access it. They were all in your—"

Enid glared at Sally.

Sally cleared her throat and continued. "But they weren't hard to work out."

"How do I read it?" asked Enid.

"Just click on the link," replied Sally.

Enid tapped the keyboard and frowned.

"I'll put it on a USB and you can print it out at the library," said Sally.

Alfred munched on a lemon butter laden scone. "She's a clever one, this one. Perhaps she could help us with our investigation?"

"No," replied Enid.

"I'll leave *The Marple Brigade* to you, Aunt Enid," said Sally.

"The Marple Brigade?" Alfred sipped his tea. "I like it. And Enid is our own Mrs Christie. Perhaps you can tell me all about this book over lunch, before *The Marple Brigade* debriefing?" He chuckled.

Mr B's ear twitched.

Enid's cup drifted forward. A dribble of coffee dripped over the edge of her teacup. Sally paused mid-sip and eyed Alfred over the rim of her cup. The corner of her mouth twitched.

"It's private," Enid croaked.

The gleam faded from Alfred's eyes. Her heart sank. She didn't like upsetting him.

"Perhaps when it's finished?" she said.

The gleam returned to Alfred's pale blue eyes. He reached for a scone.

Agnes would be livid when she found out Enid had revealed *The Book* to anyone. But it was done; she couldn't have foreseen Sally's unfortuitous discovery. The best she could do was try to minimise the damage.

"Please don't tell Agnes about the book," said Enid.

"Why not?" Sally and Alfred asked in unison.

"Um..." Yes, a good question; She'd walked right into that one. *Why indeed?* Her heart raced. She needed an excuse. She had to think quickly. "She'll be upset I was working with Olive and she was left out."

"She doesn't know about it?" asked Sally.

Enid didn't reply. She sipped her coffee; she couldn't lie to Sally, but she wouldn't quash any wrong assumptions either. And omissions weren't necessarily a lie.

"I'll not tell. I'll take your secret to my grave." Alfred placed a gentle hand on Enid's.

"Thank you, Alfred," she said.

Sally curled her feet up onto her armchair and sipped her tea. "Nor will I. We Turners must stick together."

Alfred perched on the edge of the lounge chair. "All right, we won't discuss your book, tempting though it is." He leaned closer to Enid. "I'd still like to take you to lunch tomorrow, Enid."

Enid felt Mr B's muscles tense against her leg.

"Oh, but I can't." Enid straightened her cup on the saucer. "The gardener, Simon, is coming over to look at my hydrangeas tomorrow, before our meeting - and for a little chat and scones. He's Olive's grandson, remember?"

Alfred's eyes widened. "Ah, yes. The chat." He fingered the end of his nose.

"*The Marple Brigade* investigates." Sally smiled.

Cheeky girl.

Alfred twisted the brim of his hat. "Then, how about dinner?" he asked.

Mr B rubbed hard against her leg and flicked his tail into her shins. She nudged him back. What *was* his problem? Alfred was a gentleman, with good taste in suits - even if it was high summer. But she just wasn't ready for that sort of thing. Not since Owen. She took a deep breath. Best to let him down gently.

"I'm making dinner for Sally tomorrow," she said.

"Don't worry about me, Aunt Enid," said Sally. "I've been called into work tomorrow. Several staff have called in sick. There's a bug going around. You go. Have a good time."

Enid's heart raced. "But, it's not safe." The Collector had likely gathered ten souls already; the Final Collection was drawing near. And Sally was a target.

"Oh, don't worry." Sally sipped her tea, oblivious to the danger that threatened her. "I'm on light duties and haven't needed to use the inhaler all day. And the burn *is* healing." She tugged at her top. "Much faster than expected, actually. I can hardly feel it most of the time." She patted Enid's hand.

Enid held her breath. The Dark was coming for her niece. Enid had to tell Sally of the danger, no matter what Agnes said. Some rules were made to be broken.

Enid opened her mouth and remembered: they were not alone. She bit her tongue.

"Then it's settled." Alfred jumped up to his feet, flipped his hat and planted it on his head. "I'll pick you up at six o'clock."

"No, wait. I can't..." said Enid.

"He can keep you company while I'm at work," said Sally.

Enid spun to face her niece. "Sally, I really don't think it's a good idea for you to go back to work yet."

Sally placed her cup on its saucer and looked Enid directly in the eye. "I have to go. I need the money. I can't sponge off you forever."

There was movement in the corner of Enid's eye. Alfred had slipped out of the room.

"Alfred, wait."

Enid heard footsteps in the hall.

"I'll let myself out. Thank you for the—"

There was a knock on the front door. Enid slumped back in the armchair. The document folder pressed into her back.

"What now?"

The grandmother clock's chimes echoed down the hallway. *Five o'clock.*

Enid groaned. Sally shrugged her shoulders.

"I'll get the door, shall I?" Alfred's voice drifted into the lounge room.

The front door clicked.

Enid threw her hands into the air. "By all means. It's probably Agnes wanting to know why she wasn't invited to all the fun."

"Good evening." The deep, muffled voice sounded official. "Is Miss—?" There was a pause. "Dad, what are you doing here?" The reply was barely audible.

"'Dad?'" Sally dropped her feet onto the floor and straightened up in her chair.

"Alfred's son is a police detective." Enid snatched the document folder up from the other armchair and scanned the room for a hiding place. She couldn't let Tom discover Alfred's nefarious acquisition.

Their voices grew louder as they walked down the hall. Enid shoved the folder under the armchair cushion and patted it down.

"That's a bit obvious, isn't it?" Sally closed the laptop.

Alfred walked into the room first.

"Tom..." He cleared his throat. "...that is, Detective Knowles has a few questions to ask Sally."

Enid grabbed Alfred's sleeve and ushered him into her armchair. His eyes widened as he sat. He slipped his hand down the side of its cushion.

"Shh, I don't want you to get in trouble," she whispered in his ear.

Alfred fidgeted in his seat.

Tom Knowles stepped into the room. He looked every inch the detective: clean-shaven and a precise haircut, single-breasted grey suit, and a tie his wife must have bought for him.

"I need to have a private conversation with your niece."

"Do take a seat, Detective Knowles." Enid turned to face Tom.

"Oh, *that* Miss Turner." Tom winked at Alfred.

Alfred blushed. Sally bit her lip, not hiding her smile effectively enough.

Enid escorted Tom to one end of the lounge, next to Sally's chair, and as far away from Alfred as possible.

"A cup of tea would be lovely, Miss Turner." said Tom as opened his notebook and clicked his pen.

Enid placed her palm on the side of the teapot. It was cold. *Bollocks.* Now she couldn't sit in on the interview.

"I'll fetch a cup, then." Enid picked up the teapot.

Alfred stood and followed her. As soon as they cleared the doorway, Enid pulled Alfred to one side.

"What are you doing?" she hissed. "You're supposed to be guarding the files. Do you want to get caught?"

"Don't worry I've thought of that." Alfred tapped his jacket. The document folder thudded softly.

Enid nodded and flattened herself against the wall near the doorway to listen. Alfred positioned himself against the wall beside her.

Footsteps crossed the lounge room. The door clicked shut.

"What are they saying?" asked Alfred.

"Shh, I can't hear." Enid pressed her ear against the door, struggling to hear the muffled conversation on the other side.

Mr B purred and curled his body around Enid's ankles, almost knocking her off her feet. Enid pushed him away. Mr B nudged her again, wheedling his body between her and Alfred.

"Quiet, Mr B," Enid whispered.

He pressed harder against Enid's leg and mewed loudly.

"Not now, Mr B."

His vocalisations grew louder, more intense. The voices in the lounge room stopped. Enid jumped away from the door.

"Time to make that tea, I think." She dragged Alfred into the kitchen.

Mr B padded along the carpet runner toward the kitchen. He wove across the hallway behind her heels, almost tripping Alfred, and forwent his habitual perimeter trek and remained tethered to Enid, shadowing her every move.

Enid clicked on the kettle and filled the teapot with warm water from the tap.

"How will we know what they are saying?" Alfred stepped closer to Enid.

"Not to worry." Enid swirled the teapot and smiled. "Sally will tell me everything later."

Mr B squeezed his body between them and growled.

Enid glanced out the window. She needed to distract Alfred so she could see what Mr B was trying to warn her about.

"Alfred, could you get some more sugar from the pantry, please?"

"Where is it?" he asked.

"Behind the lemon butter."

Alfred nodded and crossed to the pantry. She waited until she heard the rattle of jars.

"What's wrong, Mr B?" She glanced out the window again. The sun glared off the windscreen of Alfred's car. She frowned. "There's nothing there, silly."

Alfred hummed and trotted back to the bench with the sugar bowl.

"I thought The Fox and Firkin," he said cheerily.

Mr B head-butted Enid's leg. The kettle whistled, its shrill warble distracted her.

"Um... pardon?"

"Perfect," replied Alfred. "I've already made the booking."

"Stop fussing, Aunt Enid." Sally grabbed her car keys off the hall table and slipped her mobile phone into her sports bag.

"Are you sure they can't call someone else?" Aunt Enid leaned on her walking stick, shifting her weight as if to get a better grip. "It isn't safe out there." She peered out the door. The sun bathed her face. She seemed to relax and stood taller.

"I'll be fine." Sally slipped on her sunglasses. She was needed at the hospital. "I'll be home late tonight, after my shift."

Aunt Enid shook her head and hovered as if she wanted to say something.

Sally frowned and glanced at the wall clock near the lounge room door. It was after nine-thirty.

"I really must go, Aunt Enid, or I'll be late!" She hugged her aunt. "You enjoy your dinner date with Mr Knowles."

Aunt Enid glared at her. "It's not a date."

Sally smiled. "He seems so sweet. I like him."

"Are you sure you have to go?" Aunt Enid stared over Sally's shoulder and spoke slowly, not taking her attention from the front yard.

"Yes. And I don't want to be late." Sally turned on her heel and bustled out the front door. She paused at the edge of the porch. Storm clouds had begun to gather. She removed her sunglasses and peered into the cloud's depths. Something wasn't right...

Small crackles of lightning flickered at the top of the gloom, creeping downward with each strike until they were almost directly overhead. Sally braced herself for the oncoming peal of thunder. It would be close. Several more sparks flashed across the sky. But there was no sound.

Sally dropped her shoulders. "That's strange."

"I know." Aunt Enid's voice was suddenly very close. Her breath tickled Sally's ear.

Sally jumped and spun to face her aunt. Aunt Enid didn't flinch. She brandished her walking stick and stared at the sky, as if ready to beat back the next strike.

Mr B rushed between Sally's feet and yowled. His spiked tail was twice its normal size as if the oncoming storm's static had already struck him. Enid pushed him back with her foot.

"Inside, Mr B. This is not the time for your heroics."

The garden gnomes were gathered around Aunt Enid like a vanguard rallying around their general.

Sally edged backwards along the path toward her car; her heels knocked straggling gnomes. She faltered and struggled to keep her balance. She was surrounded.

She held her breath, sidestepped them and inched along the path toward her car, not taking her eyes off the oncoming ceramic swarm.

Her gaze darted from one gnome to the next. There were so many - so many of them. They crowded closer. Emotionless black eyes stared at her from every direction. All her nightmares had come alive!

She reeled to face the car, and was confronted by a cracked, scarlet-painted ornament - the garden gnome she had helped glue back together.

"Careful, Red," whispered Aunt Enid behind her.

"Red?" What was *it* doing here? "But you were near the chair swing?"

"Red has taken it upon himself to be your personal body guard," replied Aunt Enid in a slow, measured voice, as if calming a frightened animal.

Sally's heart raced. Her chest ached, as if hordes of faceless gnomes were already swarming over her and dragging her down. She gasped for air.

She inched a step closer to her car. The sky was darker now. The clouds had descended and skirted the treetops. She felt each silent rumble reverberate through her body, like a static charge slowly building up.

The sky shuddered with a sudden and deafening crack. The cloud parted, revealing a shimmering fissure in the sky behind it. Something writhed inside the opening. Smoke poured down. The air filled with a pungent, acrid smell.

Sally froze.

"What the—?" Her arteries felt as if they'd been injected with ice water. The sports bag slipped from her sweaty fingers and thudded onto the concrete paving. She clapped her hands over her ears. Her car keys jangled onto the ground.

"Sally!"

The scream was Aunt Enid's. Sally felt the full force of it; a throbbing wave of words barrelled into her chest. Her knees buckled. Something grabbed her from behind and dragged her back toward the house. A shadow rolled over her as two elastic-support-hosed legs straddled her body.

Silver light washed over her. She winced and struggled to keep her eyes open.

"Leave her alone!" The voice was muffled.

A grunting laugh reverberated around Sally.

The ground trembled with the sound of marching. One. Two. Converging toward her. She squirmed against the unexpected pressure of her aunt's legs, holding her still.

Sally's skin crawled, as if she could feel their cold ceramic fingers already clutching at her clothes, clawing her skin. She screamed. Out loud. For a long time.

The marching continued, not skipping a step. Closer. Closer. Her heart crashed into her stomach, making her want to vomit. Her heart palpitated - so fast. The pain crushed her chest and shot down her arm.

The laugh gurgled into silence.

Sally sucked in a sharp breath. She prised open an eyelid. Rows of ceramic gnomes marched past her, with sneers, manic grins and wild eyes - all fixed on their target.

Blood pounded in her ears. Her vision blurred. Lights flashed red through her eyelids.

Lightning crackled. She wanted to run. Her legs refused to co-operate. She tried to scream; her throat was too dry. She curled her legs up to her chest. There was nothing she could do but try to hide.

Shadows flickered around her. She imagined the painted faces rushing at her, just as she'd seen hundreds of times before, in her nightmares... But this wasn't her imagination. This was real!

A gravelly roar exploded around her. The smell of ozone grew stronger. Metal clashed. Marching feet circled, and moved away. A loud pop echoed near her head. Fragments showered over her arms like falling sand. Something bounced against her shoulder. Flecks stung her face.

Then silence.

Sally trembled. Her vision began to clear. She blinked. A smashed gnome head lay on the ground, near her cheek. She squeezed her eyes shut.

Something squirmed in her chest. It itched in her throat, growing, worming its way to escape, to rip out of her body.

Sally opened her mouth. The scream echoed around her. It rolled down the gully and bounced off the hills.

"No more!" Sally opened her eyes.

Lightning arced from the tip of the fissure, into the deepest shadow of the smoky cloud. The crack in the sky snapped shut.

The gnomes froze mid-lunge. Red was the closest. He turned to face her, his lidless eyes almost engulfing his cheeks. Even Aunt Enid stood motionless, her walking stick raised mid-air - a massive shadow looming over Sally.

The sun peeked over the top of the swirling smoke, creating a halo of fluffy hair around her great aunt's head.

She stepped forward and reached for Sally's hand. Aunt Enid's sleeve rode up her arm. A circular scar glowed faintly on her forearm. Sally hesitated.

"You have the scar too?" Sally's voice cracked. "Who are you?"

She scrambled out from between her aunt's legs. Her hands scraped on the rough edges of concrete pavers. Her fingers knocked into a gnome. She flinched and sucked in a sharp breath.

"What are *they*? All those years… the nightmares. And they were *real*! How could I not know they were real?" She stood slowly, hoping her knees would not betray her. "What have you done?"

chapter ten

"t he nightmare is always the same." A wave of sweat washed over Sally's skin. "The house is attacked by hordes of smoke-like creatures."

"The Collectors are the lieutenants of The Dark." Aunt Enid held up her walking stick defensively in front of her and searched the brightening sky.

"Then, it's all real?" Sally took a step backward.

"There is only one Collector, for now, and I plan to keep it that way. You need to get back inside. Now!"

"It's gone." Sally stood her ground and glared at the gnomes hefting scorched weapons of varying ferocity. Red stood at her feet. She shuffled another step closer to her car.

"Whose side are they on, anyway?" She grimaced. "This *can't* be real."

"Magic is real," replied Aunt Enid. "Fairies are real."

Distant thunder rumbled in the sky. Sally flinched.

"Daemons are real. They just have another name," said Aunt Enid.

"And the garden gnomes?" asked Sally. "Are they real, or just some magical... construct, like in your book?" All the things she had read in her aunt's story - alternate worlds, with fantastical armies... Sally swallowed. "It's not a novel, is it?" she asked.

Aunt Enid lowered her walking stick.

"They're my army - our army. They help defend us against the incursions from the Otherworlds."

"The Other—?" Sally shook her head. Her brain pounded. She wanted to escape, to run as fast as her feet could take her, but they refused to move.

Visions snagged at her consciousness. A red cap. A gnome. The same one that skulked at her feet now.

Sounds blended with the vision: a young girl. Her small fingers gripped a permanent marker and scribbled a name on the base of the ornament. *Red*, the girl giggled.

"Red?" whispered Sally. She snatched up the gnome.

The vision persisted. Childhood Red was unscarred. Not a blemish. The sounds intensified. Giggles became screaming and the clash of battle. The gnome's smiling eyes hardened. He raised his scythe. Darkness engulfed them.

It's dark. Sally's voice was child-like, barely a whisper. Her hand trembled.

"Don't be afraid of The Dark, Sally." Aunt Enid's voice pushed through the blackness, pulling it back. "It can only break through if we let it. And that will *not* happen today."

The darkness faded. Sally stood next to her car, a garden gnome in one hand. Her cheeks were wet. Her eyes stung. She gripped the gnome and turned it upside down. A word, in faded, child-like writing, was inscribed on each boot: *Red* on one sole, *Sally* on the other.

It was real! All of it. Sally slumped against the car bonnet.

"How could I forget?" she whispered.

Aunt Enid leaned on her walking stick. Dark circles rimmed her eyes.

"All this." Sally's fingers twitched. "This happened before? When I was a child?"

"During one of your holidays here," replied Aunt Enid.

"But why can't I remember?"

"It was thought best you forgot." Her aunt avoided her direct gaze, and took a deep breath. "The nightmares, I thought they had gone."

"No." Sally's jaw clenched. An ache crept up her cheek and tugged at her forehead. "Who thought it best I forget?" Her grip tightened on Red.

"The other Protectors. Olive. Agnes." Aunt Enid lifted her head, still avoiding direct eye contact. A furrow had etched deep between her eyes. "It isn't safe for civilians to know."

"Then how do we protect ourselves?" asked Sally.

"You don't. It's *our* job to protect you from the Otherworlds."

"Worlds?" hissed Sally. "There's more than one?"

She glared at her aunt - no longer bent over and frail. She seemed ageless, her hair immaculate, her eyes cunning, shoulders thrust back, wielding, not a stick, but a crackling weapon of silver. Her sleeves were pushed up to her elbows, ready for battle. A faint, silver line on her skin curved below the bottom of her sleeve. Sally pushed herself off the car bonnet.

"You have the scar?" The same mark she had seen on Olive and was now forming on her chest.

Her aunt dropped her arm and yanked her sleeve.

"What are you hiding?" Sally's chest tightened. The burn tingled. "How *did* I forget, Aunt Enid?"

"A memory spell." Her aunt's movements were sluggish, her voice low and devoid of emotion. "It's a simple enchantment."

"And how many times have you used it on me?"

"Just once." Aunt Enid bent over her walking stick. Her eyes remained downcast.

"You did magic on me?" Sally squeezed Red harder. The gnome squirmed but remained silent. "*You* made me forget?"

Aunt Enid edged forward a few steps. "I was trying to protect you."

Sally stepped away from her aunt. The frail old lady had returned; deep wrinkles scarred her face. Wiry hair framed her cheeks. Her eyes were a dull, dishwater grey. A stranger now stood before her. This wasn't the woman she knew. Sally's mind raced. Was this a spell too? Which was the real Aunt Enid?

"Who are you?" she hissed. "*What* are you?"

Her aunt looked haggard, more alien with each moment.

"I am who I have always been." Aunt Enid reached out her hand towards Sally.

"It's all a lie!" Sally snatched her car keys up from the ground and flung open the car door. She hurled Red onto the back seat. Her sports bag followed. "How can I trust anything you say?" She jumped into the car.

The door slammed shut as the car roared into life and jerked forward. Sally wrestled with the gearstick. The car lurched out of first gear and into reverse.

"Don't wait up for me. I'm not coming back."

"But, Sally, where will you stay? You can't go home."

"And whose fault is that? Was that to do with your Protectors as well?"

"Sally—" Her aunt hobbled towards the car.

"I have friends I can trust. I'll sleep at the hospital if I have to." Sally planted her foot onto the accelerator. Pain circled her head and lunged into her eye socket. "And keep out of my head!"

"Sally, the gate!"

Sally ignored her aunt's warning. She couldn't bear to remain here any longer. She *had* to get away.

The car boot thumped into the edge of the gate. Wood cracked and splintered. The metal hinges scraped and ground. The gate screeched open; the wood wobbled as Sally reversed past. She slammed on the brakes and spun the car onto the road.

Wheels skidded on rough gravel on the edge of the road as she gunned the engine and sped past her aunt's white picket fence, past the trees where the Collector had descended, past the truck parked at the end of the road, and turned toward the city.

She would not look back.

The grandmother clock struck six. The final gong lingered in the hallway. A knock rattled the front door. Enid's heart skipped. Sally had returned. Enid opened the door. She would have some grovelling to do, but it was worth—

Mr Knowles stood on the porch, a wide grin smothering his face. He'd changed from his 'sleuthing suit' into a well-cut blazer and bow tie. He tucked an errant wisp of hair behind his ear.

"We have a table by the—" His gaze dropped to Enid's purple fluffy slippers and frowned. "I did say six, didn't I?" He cleared his throat and removed his hat. "Oh, dear, I'm too early."

"Oh, Alfred." Enid glanced back at the clock. "I forgot." She wiped her floury hands on her apron.

Alfred's smile faded.

"Oh, no," said Enid quickly. "It's not you. I had to think. I just lost track of time, that's all. Lemon meringue pie can do that." She dusted off the remaining flour from her fingers.

"I saw your front gate." He tugged at the brim of his hat. "Hooligans, was it? I'm surprised young Simon didn't look at it while he was here."

"Simon?" Oh, dear. She'd forgotten all about the garden. She twisted the corner of her apron. "He didn't show up."

Alfred raised an eyebrow. "I would have thought him more reliable than that."

"Yes. So did I." The apron slipped from Enid's fingers.

"No need to worry. I'm sure he just got caught up on another job."

"Quite so."

"I can fix the gate before we go to dinner. I'll let Tom know about the damage."

"No, it's all right," said Enid.

"It's no trouble."

"No, really, Alfred. Your Tom will have his hands full chasing The—, our murderer."

"I'm sure he could get an officer to patrol the area." He placed his hat on the hall table. "It is their job to protect us, you know."

"It was Sally. She..." Enid lowered her head. It was her job to protect as well. Yet she had failed Sally. "It's been a horrendous day. Sally stormed out after we-" She caught her breath and reached for her walking stick in the hallstand by the front door. "We had a... disagreement," she said.

Alfred stepped forward as if to hug her. The cat flap rattled in the back door. Mr B barrelled down the hall and curled himself around Enid's legs. Alfred hesitated.

"Mr B, it's all right," said Enid. "You've met Alfred before. He's a friend."

Alfred's arms fell back to his side as he stepped away.

"I've got a toolbox in the car. I'm sure I can fix the gate before Sally gets home."

"She's not coming home." Enid bit her tongue, trying to hold back any visible emotion.

"Oh." He pointed his key at his car and pressed a button. The car chirped. He slipped the keys into his pocket. "I'm all yours. Tell me how I can help."

She wanted to tell him about The Collectors, The Dark and the danger they faced but she couldn't risk dragging Alfred in any deeper. He was an innocent, a civilian. The risk was too great - and she couldn't face explaining the whole 'protector of the world' thing. Not twice in one day. Enid shook her head.

"It's a family matter." Her shoulders slumped. "Do you mind if we don't go out to dinner? I don't think I'd be very good company."

"Righty-O." He clapped his hands together. "Sit down and you can tell me about your meeting with Agnes. That should cheer you up."

"There's nothing to tell. Agnes didn't show up for the four o'clock debriefing," said Enid. "I suppose it would have been a waste of time anyway since Simon didn't show, but she didn't know that."

"She didn't phone?" asked Alfred.

Enid shook her head.

"That's strange. She seemed keen to find out if he had any new clues."

"She's probably just pouting because she didn't get first crack at questioning him."

Everyone had abandoned her: Olive, Sally and, now, even Agnes. Enid had thought their youngest Protector had finally accepted her responsibilities but, no. Agnes had always been annoyed about her recruitment. She was undisciplined - and distracted - only ever doing what she wanted, when she wanted. Nothing had changed. And she'd chosen the worst time to abscond. It was now up to Enid to fight the oncoming Dark, with only a besotted civilian as unsuspecting back up.

She was alone.

Enid leaned all her weight onto her walking stick, still exhausted after the morning's skirmish. Mr B rubbed his cheek against her ankle and purred loudly.

"Don't worry, Enid." A gentle hand rested on her shoulder. "Let me make you dinner." Alfred's voice was soothing.

Enid raised her eyebrow. "You cook?"

"Of course I cook." He grinned. "I used to be a chef at the Hilton, you know. How about lamb in red wine, peas and mushrooms."

She licked her lips. "My favourites. How did you know?" And the ingredients were all in her pantry. Enid scoffed. "Agnes?"

Alfred just smiled. "Do you have another apron?"

"Thank you Alfred. That would be lovely." She nudged the cat away and shooed him outside, locking the latch on the cat flap.

Sally wheeled an instrument trolley along the corridor into the emergency ward.

Harsh fluorescent light bounced off the pale lino, and even paler walls. Monitors beeped regularly, behind curtained cubicles. Blue-uniformed nurses scuttled in and out of them, rattling little cups of pills and scribbling on patient records, leaving the curtains swinging behind them.

Sally shuffled her feet along the corridor. She was exhausted. It had been a long, boring shift. The Shift Supervisor had her checking medications and fetching supplies. She hadn't seen a patient all day. And eight hours was long enough to mull over the morning's events. Too long.

The burn on her chest ached. Her favourite aunt had been lying to her for... How long? She halted in the middle of the corridor. Since she was a child? Sixteen years?

If someone had told her yesterday that magic existed and creatures from fairy tales were real, she'd have laughed and marched them off to the psychiatric ward. Hell, she'd even suspected her aunt was losing it. Sally's heart clenched. Perhaps *she* was the one going crazy.

A hint of disinfectant wafted from the nearby cubicle. Sally's chest tightened. They'd lost a patient today; it affected her more than usual. She'd frozen when it happened, expecting the ceiling to open up and swallow the patient...

The Shift Supervisor looked up from her station.

"Is that one charged?" she asked gesturing at the instrument trolley.

"Yes," replied Sally.

"Good. I wish the girls on the other shift would charge them when they're done." She handed Sally a patient record. "See if you can get Mr Perkins, in number nine, to sit still long enough to take his obs."

Sally trundled the monitor trolley past the nurses station, and along the row of curtained cubicles with numbers embedded into the pale blue-flecked lino, until she reached cubicle ten.

The curtain rattled along its runners as she pulled it aside.

An elderly gentleman sat, propped up on his elevated hospital bed, mumbling to himself. His clothes had been slung over the chair. The room reeked of stale tobacco. Unhooked monitor leads jiggled as he tugged at the neck of his gown with yellow-stained fingers.

He glared at Sally. "It's been three hours since my last meds. My knee is killing me."

The smell of tobacco intensified as he spoke. Sally screwed up her nose and held her breath as she pushed the monitor behind the bedhead, checked the monitor leads hanging over the edge of the bed and plugged them into the machine.

The familiar beep filled the cubicle. Numbers climbed steadily on the readout: *140. 150. 160/95... Heartrate: 125.*

Sally noted the numbers on his chart.

"You really should give up smoking, Mr Perkins. It increases the risk of infection. I'm sure the doctor told you that after your surgery last week."

"Ha!" A cough rattled in his chest. A wave of stale tobacco smell blasted through the cubicle. "It calms me down. And I've earned it."

He shifted on the bed and scowled.

"When will I be allowed to leave? I don't want to stare at this thing all day."

He indicated the infected open wound above his knee. The surrounding skin was red and swollen. Strings of purulent discharge clung to the fascia at the edges of the exposed muscle.

Sally winced. It did look painful. She checked his chart.

"It says you only had pain killers *two* hours ago, after they cleaned the wound," she said. "You should have left the dressing on, as the doctor advised. You should know better. You've done this before."

"I haven't got time for this. I've got important things to do." He thudded his hand on the bed sheet beside him. "I want to see the doctor now. I'm in pain. And I want—"

"Good evening, Mr Perkins." The young doctor flashed a smile in Sally's direction. "He isn't giving you too much trouble, is he, nurse?"

The chart clattered on the narrow bench on the other side of the bed.

"Nothing I can't handle."

"Good. Mr Perkins has been quite feisty, today. More than usual. But then he wouldn't have such a bad infection if he'd done as he was told. Would you, Mr Perkins?"

Mr Perkins crossed his arms and harrumphed. The doctor shook his head.

"Thank you, nurse, I'll take it from here."

Sally thrust the curtain closed behind her. She gritted her teeth. She hated it when the doctors couldn't bother to use her name. He was the one who called for help, and now he didn't even trust her to continue. She plodded back to the nurse's station.

"Can you check cubicle thirteen? The nurse assigned is stuck in admission and the patient was due for her obs half an hour ago." The Shift Supervisor handed her another patient file.

Sally took it and shuffled back along the corridor to cubicle number twelve. Why hadn't Aunt Enid trusted her? And Mrs Oldham had known all along.

Two police officers sat outside the cubicle, drinking coffee. One looked up and nodded.

Sally pushed aside the cubicle curtain as she checked the chart:

Farrow, Agnes. Miss.

Sally's heart froze. Her feet refused to move.

Agnes' hair, now snow white, was pulled away from her face. A tube had been inserted down her throat to help her breathe. The monitor's beep clawed Sally's nerves.

Sally moved closer, wiping her hands with the provided alcohol gel. Agnes' face was bright red. Sally touched her palm to Agnes' forehead. It was burning hot.

Sally's hands shook as she consulted the case notes. Agnes had been admitted around lunchtime yesterday, already in a coma. She'd been attacked, with wounds to her chest and shoulder. Sally checked her obs - all stable - and took a slow, deep breath.

She stepped closer to the bed. Her hand hovered over the hospital gown. *Injuries to the chest and shoulder*; the words echoed in her mind. Was it like...?"

She pulled down the gown, just enough to reveal a thin red line circling Agnes' throat and the, now familiar, marks: two scorched bruises ringed by broken blood vessels. There were more marks under the gown. Four in all.

Sally stepped away from the hospital bed. Her stomach knotted. She'd seen those marks before. On Olive Oldham. Sally leaned on the bed rail, trying to catch her breath and quell the pain in her gut. Had Agnes' house been torched as well, like Mrs Oldham's? Like hers. She caught her breath. Sally's hand went to the bandage at her own neck. Agnes must have a necklace as well. But where was it?"

She scanned the cubicle for Agnes' personal effects and found them folded neatly on the visitor's chair. A paper bag sat on top. She checked the bag: a mobile phone with a bejewelled case, a watch and a necklace.

Sally sunk down onto the edge of the hospital bed. Metal chinked on the bed rail. She unzipped her uniform pocket and thrust her hand inside. Her fingers curled around the necklace Aunt Enid had given her

- for protection, she'd said. She pulled the necklace from her pocket and placed it next to Agnes'. They were identical but for the precious stone at the centre. Hers was a sapphire, Agnes' was a ruby.

Sally's head swam.

Did this make her one of *them*? Was she marked for death too? Was that why the Collector was after her?

Her hand hovered above the rubbish bin; she let the necklace dangle from her fingers and hesitated. Aunt Enid said it was for her protection. Now Aunt Enid had brought the hordes of hell down on her. Perhaps she *did* need protecting? She drew the necklace back up into her palm.

Two similar attacks *could* be a coincidence, but three? It explained why the police officer had asked so many questions. Someone was targeting old women. No wonder her aunt was so concerned with missing persons. And he must suspect Sally's attack was connected as well.

Would the killer go after Aunt Enid as well? She could protect herself - Sally had witnessed that - but she was looking frail when Sally had left. What if the Collector-daemon attacked while her aunt was still weak?

Sally jumped to her feet; she had to protect her aunt! She pressed the necklace into Agnes hand and checked her watch. *Five past nine.* Twenty-five minutes till her shift ended. She paced the cubicle. She had to get back to her aunt's as soon as possible.

Aunt Enid was in danger.

The mouth-watering aroma of red wine and mushrooms tickled Enid's nostrils. She breathed it in slowly, savouring each mouthful as she stalked a pea around her plate.

She eyed Alfred, at the opposite end of the dining table, as he tucked into his lamb. She slid the pea into her mouth and bit into its flesh. The flavour burst over her tongue. Perfect.

"You're an excellent cook, Alfred." She loaded up her fork with the last of her food. "It was absolutely delicious. Did you really work at the Hilton?"

Alfred nodded. "In my younger days."

Enid smiled. "I bet you'd have some stories to tell?"

"Yes." He placed his knife and fork on his plate. "But they are not *mine* to tell."

Enid raised an eyebrow.

"Secrets are like promises," he said, "they are made to be honoured."

"I assure you I'm very good at keeping secrets."

"I'm afraid you can't tempt me, Enid Turner." He grinned. "All my secrets will go with me to the grave."

Enid lowered her fork slowly. He could cook *and* keep secrets. Perhaps she *could* trust him? Even Protectors need assistance; why else would Agnes push him in her direction?

A gentle tap on the window caught Enid's attention. A pair of yellow eyes reflected back from the other side of the dining room window. They blinked.

Poor Mr B. She just couldn't fathom why he'd taken a disliking to Alfred. He was usually such a good judge of character. But Agnes had vouched for Alfred, and she rarely admitted outsiders to her circle of acquaintances.

Enid bit her lip. The taste of red wine brushed her tongue. She licked her lips. He was a *very* good cook.

Mr B tapped the window again. Enid shook her head.

"You stay outside until you can behave yourself when we have guests." She glanced at the police file on the table in front of her. A small spiral notebook rested on top of it. She slid her dinner plate to one side, dragged the file closer and opened it.

Only three more souls and The Dark would have enough souls to break through. At least that's what Olive told her. And if all the missing people were taken by the Collector...

She spread out the files and counted them.

No, two! It only needed two more. Enid remembered a reference she'd found in Olive's *Book*: The Dark consumed its final soul on leaving the Otherworld and entering our world. She shuffled the files back into a pile.

"Are you sure this was all of them?" she asked. "Nine missing people, in less than a month?"

Alfred craned his neck to view the files.

"I think you'd be more comfortable here." Enid pulled out the dining chair next to her.

"Yes, and mostly in the Hills or foothills," Alfred moved closer and examined the papers.

"Did your Tom mention anything about Olive or the investigation?"

Alfred sat back in his chair. "No. He wondered why I was being so nosey and told me it was 'police business'. Then he lectured me about the risks for the amateur sleuth."

Enid thrummed her fingers on the dining room table.

"He said I should I should try to impress my lady friends with dinner, not a show."

Enid's fingers halted mid-thrum.

Alfred cleared his throat. "By not playing detective."

"Ah, I see." Enid let her remaining fingers fall onto the table. "So we'll have to do it on our own, then?"

"Do what?" Alfred's cheeks flushed.

"Sleuthing, my dear Alfred." She patted him on the hand.

Mr B growled outside the window.

"Hush, Mr B. Go play with Red." She re-stacked the photocopied notes. "Now, if only Simon hadn't stood me up this afternoon." She opened the small notebook. "He could have answered some of my questions." She sighed. "I'll have to chase that up on Monday, before Agnes decides she wants to beat me to it." She sighed. "I made a fresh batch of scones this afternoon too. I suppose I'll have to make another batch before then."

Enid scribbled a reminder in the notebook: *Question Simon Oldham.*

"I do wish Agnes had come this afternoon. I tried to phone her but she didn't answer." This had been Agnes' first real test as a Protector, and she had let the side down.

"I'm sure she had a good reason," said Alfred.

"But there's so much to do. We needed to work out our plan of attack."

"Let's start by listing everything we know so far." Alfred gently took the pen from Enid's hand and slid the notebook in front of him. "We know there are nine missing people, right?"

"And a murder," replied Enid.

Alfred nodded and scribbled in the notebook: *nine missing. One murder.*

Enid took a deep breath and listed their clues. "There's Olive's break-in and Sally's house fire. Oh, and the footprints near Olive's back door." Enid tapped the notebook. "Make sure you write that down."

Alfred jotted it down. Enid made a mental note of the soot on the fly screens and in the beehive, but didn't mention them to Alfred. She could add them in later.

"The arson at Sally's." She paused, before her voice betrayed her feelings, and took a deep breath. "And her attack."

"And her smashed-in door," added Alfred.

"Yes."

"What about Sally's burns?" asked Alfred. "Tom seemed very interested in them. I gather Olive had similar injuries? That's what prompted his investigation."

"Really?"

Alfred nodded and finished off the list. He paused and lifted the pen.

"Do you think it's a pyromaniac?" he asked.

Enid didn't answer.

His eyes widened.

"And the vandalism: all the garden gnomes, the shed break in..." He chewed the end of the pen. "I wonder if Tom could identify the footprints near Mrs Oldham's back door?" He completed the list and passed the notebook back to Enid.

His handwriting was precise and confident. Her heart fluttered. It reminded Enid of her Owen's handwriting. Tears rimmed her eyes.

Alfred placed his hand on hers. "Don't worry, Enid. Tom will find the culprit."

"You write like Owen," she whispered.

"Who?"

"A friend I... lost. A long time ago." Enid closed her eyes. She could see Owen's jaunty moustache, his blue eyes. He had looked so handsome in his uniform. Her eyes flickered open. Worry lines rimmed Alfred's pale blue eyes - the same colour as Owen's.

"Oh, I'm sorry." Alfred leaned back in his chair and stared at the notebook. "I didn't know."

"We all have a past, Alfred. Our secrets." Enid retrieved the notebook. "I'm sure you turned a few heads in your day."

Alfred smiled. "Now, that would be telling. And a gentleman doesn't—"

"Kiss and tell?" Enid winked.

Alfred cleared his throat. "Never." His little finger brushed her hand on the table.

The front door flew open.

Mr B disappeared from the windowsill. Enid could hear his feet racing down the hall. He skidded into the dining room and leapt onto the table.

Alfred's hand flinched away from Enid's.

"Mr B, manners!" Enid jumped to her feet.

Sally appeared in the dining room doorway. Her sports bag clattered onto the hall tiles. Her face was flushed, her eyes darted around the room, stared out the window and locked on Enid's.

"That daemon thing," she gasped, "The Collector. It attacked Aunt Agnes. She's in a coma."

chapter eleven

nid couldn't shake the feeling of guilt. She should have checked why Agnes hadn't come over yesterday. Her hand shook as she sipped her tea.

"What is going on, Enid?" asked Alfred.

Enid and Sally sat on one side of the dining table, facing Alfred. Unwashed plates were still piled on the table between them.

"I want to know what happened to Aunt Agnes." Sally crossed her arms and glared at Enid.

"Aunt Agnes?" Alfred placed his hand on Sally's arm. "I'm so sorry. I didn't realise you were related."

"No, she's Aunt Enid's friend," said Sally. "I've known her all my life. Well, at least I thought I did."

Alfred stared at her, his mouth open. Enid frowned. She didn't have a choice now; Alfred had to be told.

"I think I need to tell you both the truth," she said.

Mr B circled the chair on her other side, jumped up and glared at Alfred, as he settled himself on the seat.

"Yes, you do," said Sally.

Mr B had fallen asleep, having lost interest in the conversation around midnight.

The hall clock chimed three times. *The Hour of the Wolf.* Enid's fingers tensed. She peered out the window. Stars glinted in the clear sky and the moon skimmed the treetops. There was no sign of the Collector. Her fingers relaxed.

Enid pulled her sleeve down to cover her scar. Would Alfred believe her, or would he consider them *both* mad? She held her breath, hoping she hadn't lost an ally. With Agnes out of action, she needed all the help she could get.

Alfred shook his head, avoiding her gaze. He remained silent.

Sally frowned and shifted in her chair.

"So, you're saying it's real?" Alfred examined the police file in front of him and tapped the papers with his finger. "And the missing people? That was the work of a daemon?"

"A Collector," Enid let the breath escape slowly.

"From an alternate world?"

"Yes. We call it the Otherworld."

"And these Collectors are the vanguard to an invasion by The Dark?"

"Not if I can stop it," replied Enid.

"And it collects souls?" asked Alfred.

"Yes, it needs their energy to crack the protective shell of this world."

"It was responsible for Mrs Oldham's murder?" he asked. "And the attacks on Sally and Agnes?"

"Yes."

Enid felt sorry for him. The poor man looked shell-shocked. It was a lot of information to take in at once.

"Would you like a cup of tea, Alfred?" she asked.

Alfred dragged his gaze back to Enid. He leaned back in his chair, opened his mouth and blinked.

"Or perhaps something stronger?"

He nodded slowly.

Enid retrieved a cut-crystal decanter of brandy and a glass from the side cabinet. She poured him a drink, and hesitated. He was pale. She poured him a double, left the decanter on the table in front of him and sat back down in her chair.

Alfred sipped it slowly.

"And your manuscript..." asked Sally, "and '*The Book*' on Mrs Oldham's computer?"

"Aren't part of a novel," replied Enid. "It's a journal, a record of our research and dealings with the Otherworld. All three of us have one."

"Is that why the entries are all dated?" asked Sally.

Enid nodded.

"Were your grandmother or mother Protectors as well?"

"Why do you ask?" said Enid.

"I recognised your mother's writing from the family recipe book."

Enid bit her lip and nodded slowly.

"It's not hereditary, is it?" asked Sally.

"Not as far as I know," replied Enid.

"Then why wasn't I given a choice? Sally tugged at the bandage covering the burn on her chest. "Why have I got this?"

"It's from the magic of the amulet when it transfers its allegiance to the next Protector."

"Magic? Why am I not surprised?" Alfred gulped down his drink, poured himself another double brandy and drained the glass again.

"The amulet chooses the recipient," said Enid. "None of us had a choice."

"That's a bit old fashioned, isn't it?" asked Sally.

Enid ignored Sally's remark.

"As far as we know, the amulet allies itself to us, so we can channel magic."

"As far as you know?" Sally sat upright in her chair. "You don't know for sure?"

"We weren't given instructions. That's why we write *The Books*. We chronicle everything we learn, so we don't forget, and we can pass it onto those who come after us."

"So you, Agnes, and Sally, are Protectors?" asked Alfred.

"I didn't say I was," replied Sally. "I just came back to make sure Aunt Enid was safe." Her chair scraped as she stood. "And we can't sit around all night. Aunt Agnes has been attacked."

"Agnes is safe where she is. Collectors won't attack in a public place. They prefer to work in secret, with no witnesses."

"So," said Sally. "Just how many of these Protectors are there? And why aren't they here backing you up now Aunt Agnes is hurt?"

"Each crossing point has one Shield of Protectors. Each Shield has three Protectors. There are only ever three at one time. And, no, we don't have 'back up'."

"Why?" asked Sally.

"We don't know," replied Enid. "It's just how it is."

"I can see why Aunt Agnes gets pissed off with it all." Sally huffed. "We have to stop it coming after us. We can't stay holed up here forever."

"Magic has a cost. It needs to regain its strength before its next attack. So we are safe, for now. They can't cross the Wards; the fence is made of hawthorn and gnomes are always on guard. They'll let us know if anything stirs." A smile flickered over Enid's lips. "And I have a few tricks up my sleeve. We will be ready, I promise."

"Are you sure about that?" Sally crossed her arms.

Enid's heart sank. Agnes had warned her about Sally's potential reaction.

"I didn't mean to drag you into this. I thought it would protect you." Enid placed her hand on Sally's arm.

Sally flinched. Enid's hand snapped back.

"I'm so sorry, Sally." Her heart twisted in her chest to think she'd caused her niece such pain.

"It's okay, Aunt Enid." Sally blew gently on her skin. It was bright red. "The sunburn is worse than I thought. That's all."

Enid suspected it was part-truth, but it didn't convince her enough to quell her feelings of guilt. Perhaps removing the superficial discomfort would soothe Sally's pain.

"Let me help you," whispered Enid. She glanced at Alfred. "You might want another one after this."

The decanter clinked on the edge of his glass as Alfred poured another drink.

Enid steeled herself for the task; she was still physically exhausted from the previous morning's battle. She placed her hand on Sally's forearm. The centre of Enid's palm tingled. Warmth spread over her hand and radiated along her fingers. The tips buzzed with energy, sparks crackling around them.

Alfred's pupils widened, rimmed with only a sliver of pale blue iris. He gulped another mouthful of brandy.

Sally's muscles tensed under Enid's palm. A frown flashed over her forehead.

"Try to relax, Sally," whispered Enid.

Sally took a deep breath. The muscles relaxed slightly. The redness faded to pink, first on her forearm. It crept up her arm and across her chest and neck. Sally's arm relaxed onto the table. The frown ebbed from her forehead as she wriggled her fingers and bent her arm. A faint smile flickered over her lips.

Enid eased back into the dining chair, exhausted, barely able to keep her eyes focused.

Sally checked under the bandage on her chest. Her smile faded.

"Ah, I'm afraid that is beyond my abilities," said Enid. "It has to heal on its own. It will only take a couple of days."

"Blimey." Alfred plopped his glass on the table. "Miss Marple has nothing on you!"

He poured himself another drink. His fourth glass - two of which were doubles. Enid raised an eyebrow and held out a shaky hand.

"I think you'd better hand over your keys, Alfred. You're not driving home tonight. Sally will make up the guest room for you."

The morning sunlight trickled through the kitchen curtains and reflected off the melamine bench tops, accentuating each scratch and blemish accumulated over five decades of use.

Enid had shuffled into the kitchen to find Alfred had washed and put away the cooking pots and set two more places for breakfast. The delicious aroma of mushroom, tomato and shallot omelette, hot toast and fresh-brewed coffee still filled the room.

She poured coffee into her favourite teacup and glanced out the window.

Alfred leaned out of his car window and waved a USB in the air. Enid raised an eyebrow. She was impressed; his shirt and jacket were immaculate, with barely a crease. She watched his car drive off along the road toward Adelaide.

Mr B padded into the kitchen, lapped the room perimeter, purred and trotted back out into the hallway. Human footsteps thudded on the tiles in the hall. Sally yawned, her eyelids heavy, as she entered the room. She slapped on the kettle and slumped onto a chair.

"You'll be late for work," said Enid.

Sally shook her head. "Jen said she'd cover my next two shifts. You're stuck with me for a few days. I thought you'd need some help." She sniffed the omelette on her plate. "That smells delicious, Aunt Enid."

"It wasn't me, dear." Enid sipped her coffee. "It's all Alfred's work."

"He cooks?" Sally licked her lips, plunged her fork into the omelette and took a bite. "Can we keep him?"

Enid didn't reply. It was bad enough having Agnes insist on playing matchmaker. She didn't want to encourage Sally as well.

Sally finished her breakfast, drank her tea, then rested her elbows on the table and sank her forehead into her hands.

"You look terrible," said Enid.

"I couldn't sleep."

"More nightmares?"

Sally nodded.

Guilt tugged at Enid's gut. She should have never meddled with Sally's memory, never listened to Olive. Magic was capricious. One could never predict the consequences.

"I'm so sorry. I didn't—"

"It's all right, Aunt Enid." Sally sat up in the chair. "It wasn't the gnomes this time. It was you."

"Me?" Enid gripped the handle of her teacup. Did Sally hate her for what she'd done?

"The nightmares have changed. The Collector is attacking you. That's why I came back. I can't let them take you."

Enid grip loosened on the teacup.

"Then we'd better start fortifying our defences for battle."

"What do I have to do?" Sally straightened her shoulders. The spark returned to her eyes.

Enid was already in the pantry, collecting jars of lemon butter.

"How good is your throwing arm?" she asked.

"I used to be pitcher in the school softball team, if you remember. I'm a bit rusty though." Sally stood in the pantry doorway, a quizzical look on her face. "Why?"

The jars clinked as Enid thrust them into Sally's arms.

"Are we going to scone them back to the Otherworld, with tangy condiments?" she chuckled.

"No, and don't be cheeky." Enid placed another jar on top of the pile in Sally's arms. "Acid burns them." Enid held up one of the jars. It glowed yellow in the sunlight. "Think of these as Molotov cocktails. Just smash one of these on its head."

"But lemon butter doesn't burn."

"It doesn't take much. Collectors don't like *anything acidic*. They use Adelaide as a crossing point because of the alkaline soil. The soil here makes the property one of the most alkaline places in the Hills. The cottage was built of sandstone to discourage them. And a Protector was placed to guard it." She handed the jar to Sally.

"So, it's like a hellmouth?"

Enid frowned. "A what?"

"Never mind." Sally placed the jars on the kitchen table and returned to the pantry.

"Any small trace will ward them off. Even changing the pH of the soil can help deter them."

"Ah, the hydrangeas! That's why they're blue and not pink. You use them like litmus paper, to make sure the soil isn't alkaline?"

"Exactly."

"Wasn't the gardener supposed to come yesterday to fix the hydrangeas?" asked Sally.

"He didn't turn up," replied Enid.

"That's strange."

"I know." Enid nodded. "No apology. No explanation."

"No, not that." Sally shook her head. "I was sure..." Her shoulders dropped. A jar shifted, with a clink. "I thought I saw his ute at the end of the road when I left yesterday." She adjusted the jar on top of the pile. "I must've been mistaken. I was a bit distracted."

Enid looked out the window and made a mental note to ask Alfred if he'd seen the vehicle, either on the way up the hill last night or on his errand this morning.

A jar slipped from Sally's arm and shattered on the floor. Yellow oozed from the broken jar and along the tiles.

"The broken jar of lemon butter in Mrs Oldham's kitchen..." Her eyes widened. "She was trying to defend herself from the Collector that attacked her, wasn't she?" asked Sally.

"Yes." Enid passed Sally a second load of jars. "Pile these near the windows and doors, anywhere you may get a clear shot. I'll get the tea trolley from the laundry. We can use it to move the remaining jars to where they are needed."

Sally stared at the jars in her arms.

"Lickety-split, girl. There's a lot more to do yet."

The cotton sheet wafted down over the standing mirror in Sally's bedroom. It clung to the frame and fell in deep folds around its base.

The back screen door flapped shut.

Sally picked up the remaining folded sheets and ducked into the hall. A tea trolley squeaked down the hallway as Aunt Enid wrestled with its warped, rust-flecked frame. One of the wheels wobbled mid-air as she pushed it into the kitchen.

"Aunt Enid?"

Her aunt glanced up. Sally hesitated. Her aunt's eyes had lost their mischievous glint. Instead, they were that of a battle-hardened soldier - simultaneously ready for attack, and exhausted from the fight. She'd seen that look before, when she'd worked at the Repatriation Hospital. The moment was fleeting. Once again, dear sweet Aunt Enid, stood before her.

"Yes, dear." Her aunt's voice was quiet and calm. She turned and trotted down the hall toward Sally.

"Why do we need to cover the mirrors?" Sally leaned against the doorframe.

"So the Collectors can't use them," said Aunt Enid.

It *sounded* crazy, but Sally knew better after everything she'd seen recently.

"I don't understand."

"Traditionally it's so the spirits of the dead can't travel back to our world."

"More wives' tales?"

"Have you learnt nothing?" Enid slapped her hand gently. "It's to stop nasty things from the Otherworld, like the Collectors or The Dark, from entering. A mirror is like a bridge."

Aunt Enid took one of the sheets, led Sally into the spare bedroom and draped it over the wardrobe mirror, tucking the edges in tight.

"The Protectors have been fighting Otherworld incursions for millennia. Each culture in its own way, creating its own legends, but all are based in fact. They've just got distorted over the years."

"Like the bees?" asked Sally.

"Yes, like the bees."

"The Collector can travel via mirrors?"

Enid nodded.

"Then why are we waiting?" Sally yanked the sheet off the mirror. "Let's use the mirrors to go after them? The best offence is a quick attack, after all."

"Actually, the best offence is a good defence," said Aunt Enid. "And we can't use the mirrors. Only Travellers can enter the Otherworlds."

"So, The Dark is a Traveller?"

"Technically, no. It harnesses the energy of creatures' souls to create a bridge."

"Like a vampire?" Sally's heart froze. Were vampires real?

"You could say that," replied Aunt Enid. "It consumes the energy and uses it to make cracks between the worlds."

"The lightning? The crack in the sky yesterday morning? That was The Dark trying to get through?"

"Yes."

"The storm in the cemetery, and the birds? That was The Dark? Was it trying to steal Mrs Oldham's soul?"

Her aunt's nostrils flared. Her eyelids narrowed. "Cemeteries are out of bounds. They are sanctuary for souls, as are churches. It knew that,"

Aunt Enid growled. "It should not have been there. It tried to bend the rules, and failed." She stared out the window. "But it only needs three more souls to break through. Until then, we have only the Collectors to worry about." Aunt Enid collected up the sheet and replaced it over the wardrobe mirror. "And they use mirrors."

"Now, cover the mirror in my bedroom and pour the coffee grounds in the front garden. Alfred should be back with the printout of Olive's *Book* soon, and then we've got a fence to fix."

The sun was low in the sky. The thud of a hammer rang through the front yard. A hot wind shook the branches of the lemon tree. Enid's muscles tensed. She glanced across the yard. Her gnome regiment remained motionless. All waiting and watching: Winky, Cottontop, Boots, Snow...

"Red?" she whispered. She scanned the area under the lemon tree near the swing chair. "Where are you?"

The gully wind strengthened. Enid gripped her walking cane and sniffed the air. Nothing but eucalyptus and dust. Her muscles relaxed. It was *just* a breeze.

"Only a few more to go." Alfred stood upright and smiled.

Enid tested the replacement hawthorn paling. The gate rattled. The paling didn't budge.

"Excellent, Alfred. That should keep them out for a while," she said.

"It's an odd choice of wood for a picket fence," said Alfred.

"Hawthorn?" Enid smiled. "It's been used for protection for generations."

She stepped back and examined the wood, with its tell-tale twisting patterns of pale cream, brown and red. Occasional cracks and knotholes scarred the boards. The rest of the palings were also hawthorn, but painted white to disguise their origin. The new wood stood out in contrast.

Enid sighed. The defence was now visible to their enemy. No doubt they would soon find a way around it. But she was doubtful they would wait until then. The portents only aligned once every few generations. The year's soaring temperatures had triggered an unscheduled incursion - the world only had itself to blame for that - and it ended with the next full moon, in three days.

No, it was now or wait at least another sixty years. Its course was set, and it was perilously close to succeeding.

"Not on my watch," whispered Enid through gritted teeth.

Alfred adjusted his work gloves, placed another paling against the gate's wooden frame and drove the hammer home with a crack. The gate shuddered.

"How's it going?" asked Sally. Cups rattled on the drinks tray she carried. "I thought you might need a cuppa. Tea with two sugars for you, isn't it, Alfred?"

"Excellent." Enid picked up her coffee and sipped it.

"Pop mine on the table, please, Sally," said Alfred. "I'm almost done."

Sally placed the tray on the small table under the lemon tree, sat on the swing chair and sipped her iced tea.

A melodic tune erupted in Sally's pocket. She answered her mobile phone, frowned and rose slowly from the chair. The conversation was inaudible.

"What's wrong?" Enid balanced her teacup on the gatepost and hurried to join Sally under the lemon tree to hear the conversation.

"It's about Aunt Agnes." Sally slipped the phone back into her pocket. " Jen said she regained consciousness last night."

"That's good isn't it?" asked Alfred as he rammed another nail home.

"Aunt Agnes has left the hospital." Sally shook her head. "She signed herself out this morning."

"Can she do that?" Alfred straightened his back, stretched and wiped his forehead with the back of his hand. "Don't they have to keep her in for observation or something?"

"Jen says she's made a remarkable recovery. The doctors can't explain it. Aunt Agnes must have a tough head."

"A thick head, more like," said Enid.

"Well, she insisted they let her go, threatened lawyers. All her results were normal, so they couldn't keep her there."

"Typical," said Enid. "She never listens to advice."

"But where will she go?" asked Sally. "She can't go home. The police said there was a fire at her house too."

As if on cue, the sound of an approaching car caught their attention. A taxi turned the corner and drove along the road toward them. Its wheels crunched on the gravel driveway.

Alfred opened the patchwork gate. The taxi parked in the driveway. The back door opened.

Agnes emerged from the taxi and stepped onto the crazy paving. Her face was gaunt, her cheeks flushed. Any remnant of fading red hair had gone. It was now snow white and glowed in the sun.

Enid stepped forward to assist Agnes, but said nothing about her precious, once-fiery, locks.

Agnes blinked and, for a moment, her eyes locked on Enid's face. "Thank you," she whispered.

She took a few tentative steps. She paused and turned her head, as if scanning the yard, her eyes not keeping pace with her head movement. Her legs wobbled.

Enid rushed to Agnes' side, cradled Agnes' head in her hand, and examined her eyes. The irises were dull and her pupils didn't react to the light.

Enid bit her lip. Agnes had retreated into herself. Enid remembered Olive warning them of the dangers of using too much magic as Agnes' predecessor, Sylvia, had done. Enid swallowed. Magic always had a cost.

"Is this it?" asked the taxi driver.

"Hmmm?" was Agnes' only reply.

"Yes. Thank you for bringing our Agnes home. We'll look after her now. Thank you," said Enid. "How much do we owe you?"

Alfred snapped to attention. "Here, let me get that." He stepped forward, produced his wallet and handed the driver some bills.

Sally joined them. "Are you okay, Aunt Agnes?"

Agnes didn't reply.

Alfred closed the gate behind the taxi and joined them.

"Shouldn't she still be in hospital?" he asked.

"They can't help. She's drained all her magic," replied Enid. "Her mind has retreated to recover. I suppose it would appear like a coma to traditional doctors. She just needs rest to recover the energy. I've got some herbs that will help. But it will take time."

"Do we have enough time? Will she be okay before the Collector returns?" asked Sally.

Enid stared into Agnes' eyes again. Enid's lip twitched nervously.

"I'm not sure," she said after a long pause.

It was the calm before the storm, except Enid had no idea when the storm would break. There was that sense of anticipation, tinged with adrenaline and laced with fear. It suffocated her.

Enid stirred the contents of the saucepan. The smell of tangy lemon butter bubbled up from the wood stove. More double saucepans simmered away on the stovetop, almost ready to boil.

She had spent all day in the kitchen, making lemon butter, having sent Sally to collect every remaining lemon on, in, or around the old tree in the front yard.

Alfred had made himself comfortable in the lounge room, a glass of port in one hand, Olive's Book in the other trying to discover any record of a weakness in the Collector they could use to their advantage. Reconnaissance, he called it. Nosey, Agnes would have said.

Mr B constantly prowled the internal cottage perimeter, stopping to glare out each window as he made his endless rounds.

Sally had fallen back on her role as nurse and carer, insisting Agnes get rest. Agnes, of course, refused to comply and had escaped her bedroom to wander aimlessly around the cottage, mumbling to herself with only flashes of coherency.

The refrigerator door slammed shut. Enid spun around, waving the wooden spoon in the direction of the noise.

"It's never the ones you suspect," grumbled Agnes under her breath.

"What isn't, dear?" asked Enid.

Agnes stared past her, shook her head and wandered back into the hallway towards the front door.

Sally rushed past the kitchen door and chased Agnes down the hallway.

Hot lemon butter dripped onto Enid's hand. She licked the grainy mixture. The sugar still wasn't dissolved. She sighed and stirred the mixture faster.

Sally returned several minutes later and collapsed into one of the kitchen chairs.

"I think I've settled her again," she said. "I caught her staring at the hall clock muttering about running out of time. She chased Mr B outside earlier. I think she tried to put him in the washing machine. I thought I'd see if she'd sit still long enough for a cup of tea."

"I think a cuppa is an excellent idea." Enid poured the batch of lemon butter into the jars on the table. "I think there's still some coffee in the machine."

Sally flicked on the kettle, poured Enid a cup and ducked into the pantry.

"Where's the sugar bowl, Aunt Enid?" Sally's voice echoed out of the pantry.

"Should be in the pantry," replied Enid.

Sally popped her head out. "I can't see it."

"Just milk will be fine then." Enid placed the lids loosely on each jar and returned to the stove for the next batch.

Sally opened the refrigerator door and sighed. "I found the sugar."

The teaspoon clinked on the side of Enid's teacup.

"Aunt Agnes will recover, won't she?" asked Sally.

"Eventually." Enid placed the saucepan on the wooden cutting board next to the jars. "It's different for each Protector. Agnes doesn't have a Focus, so she can't channel energy from around her. She prefers to do it all herself. As always."

"Focus?" asked Sally.

"A magic wand or a staff. It helps to syphon energy from the things around us, even the air," said Enid. "Collectors use lightning - electrical energy - pulling it directly from the sky. I have my walking stick. It does the same thing." Enid chuckled. "And no one thinks twice about a little old lady and her walking stick. Show people what they expect. It puts them off their guard." She grinned.

The kettle whistled.

"Did I hear the kettle?" Alfred sauntered into the kitchen, reading spectacles perched on the end of his nose, the print out of *The Book* in the other and a worried look on his face. He sat at the kitchen table and opened *The Book* to a dog-eared page. "You need to hear this."

"What have you found?" Enid sat down next to Alfred.

"The final soul to be consumed by The Dark..." he hesitated.

"Oh, just tell us, please, Alfred." Enid crossed her arms.

"I think you both may want something stronger than caffeine." Alfred swallowed. "The last soul must be that of a Protector."

The sun lounge creaked as Sally wriggled into the well-worn dent in the chair. She struggled to keep her eyes open in the heat. Alfred had made a delicious breakfast, of which she'd overindulged. But she had no regrets. She'd spent most the day chasing Aunt Agnes down the hallway before finally convincing her to rest.

Aunt Enid had urged Sally to get some rest before the Collector returned.

A breeze danced around her ankles. Sally took a deep breath and let her body sink further into the sun lounge. She was exhausted.

A hot gully breeze swept through the craggy line of hawthorn bushes along the back fence. They swayed and twisted like an animated forest in a fairy tale. A shiver crawled down Sally's back. They were an unlikely-looking ally. Even the bees avoided them when they were in flower.

She fidgeted in the chair.

They were safe, for now, holed up behind magical wards while the Collector stalked its remaining souls.

She wanted to take the fight to the Collector, prevent it from killing more innocents but, unless they discovered the identity of the Collector's current host, they had no way of knowing who would be next. What was certain was that it would come for them. And it would be soon enough.

Sally's stomach sank. Aunt Enid had been furious Mrs Oldham hadn't told them the Dark needed the soul of a Protector to complete the crossing. The words stirred up dread. Sally's heart pounded heavily in her chest. *A Protector.* Any one of them. She struggled to breathe. *Me!*

She reached for her iced tea and sipped it slowly as she scanned the back yard, and took long, slow breaths. She longed for something stronger but needed to keep her mind clear.

Bees floated on the wind, hovering near her ear, buzzing excitedly about their latest travels, and flew off. A cheeky worker buzzed her nose and flew around the side of the house, past Alfred's car, now parked near the laundry, and into the front yard.

From where she lay, she could see the repaired front gate. The gnomes had gathered along the fence. Sally's breath faltered. She took another sip, and regretted she hadn't poured herself a glass of white wine instead. *The gnomes were on their side.*

"Gnomes are my friends," she whispered to herself.

"It's coming!" Agnes' scream echoed through the yard.

The screen door slapped against the doorframe. Sally swore under her breath.

Alfred trotted across the back yard to his car. He tipped his hat in Sally's direction. He fiddled with his keyring, as if checking something, smiled and pressed the key fob's unlock button. The car's lights flashed and chirped.

"What's all the commotion?" asked Sally.

"It was Agnes. She had a nightmare."

"Poor Aunt Agnes. Is she okay?"

Alfred nodded. "Your aunt is with her now." He opened the car door. "Oh, could you tell her I've popped down the Hill to fetch something that may help. I'll be back in an hour, then I'll start lunch."

Sally nodded, licked her lips and wondered what gastronomic delights he had in store for them this time. She checked the time on her phone.

"Don't be long." She waved him off and snuggled back into the sun lounge determined not to think of the oncoming battle.

Alfred unlatched the gate and reversed his car up the empty driveway; the gnomes had rushed toward the commotion in the cottage. The sole remaining garden gnome dodged from the path of the car as Alfred drove away.

Sally jumped.

"The gnomes will protect me," she whispered. She had to accept Aunt Enid's guard gnomes were there to protect them. "They're on our side." She took a long, deep breath. "The bees will warn me of danger."

A bee rested on her shoulder, its wings tickled her neck.

"Won't you?" she whispered.

It buzzed in affirmation and lifted off.

Sally felt her chest rise and fall.

The gnomes will protect me. The bees will warn me.

She concentrated on slowing her breaths and repeated the mantra.

The gnomes will protect me. The bees will warn me.

She closed her eyes and began her familiar routine to reduce her anxiety, searching for far away sounds: the drone of traffic on the main road on the other side of the hill, a sputtering lawn mower. Cockatoos screeched in the scrub beyond the hawthorn hedge. Magpies serenaded the lowering sun. Rosellas chittered in the lemon tree. Ravens cawed in the nearby trees and flapped overhead.

They keep watch, Aunt Enid had said.

Sally took another deep breath and counted to ten. Her muscles slowly relaxed. She was safe within her aunt's wards.

She re-focused on the sounds. Closer. Centring herself.

Shadows flitted across her closed eyelids. A loud flapping rattled her glass. Sally twitched and cracked open an eyelid, straightened her back and scanned the yard.

Nothing.

She repeated the mantra: *The gnomes will protect me. The bees will warn me. The ravens keep watch.*

She closed her eyes and searched for sounds. Bees buzzed. Leaves hissed in the wind.

A hot wind scorched her bare toes. They twitched. *Bollocks!* She'd forgotten to put on sunscreen again. Aunt Enid would never let her hear the end of it.

"Concentrate on the sounds. Don't be distracted." She filled her lungs with air, feeling it warm her body. "Just relax."

The ravens flapped closer, fanning her face. Shadows flickered across her closed eyelids again. She waved her hand in their direction and focused on her breathing, her heartbeat, and ignored the surrounding distractions and tuned out the bees.

A shadow moved across her closed eyelids. A heavy weight fell on her shoulder. And everything went silent.

chapter twelve

S orry to bother you, dear," said Enid.

Sally sat upright on the sun lounge. Her elbow knocked the empty glass, smashing it onto a concrete paver. She glared at Enid.

"Oh, let me clean that up before you step on it," said Enid.

Sally shook her head. "I'll do it."

"You forgot your hat again." Enid tsked. "It's a miracle you're not burnt to a crisp."

She shook her head and squinted in the direction of the mid-morning sun. Its heat clung to her skin. There was no breeze. No gnomes. Nothing. The yard was silent. Even the birds had abandoned their endless flitting and chittering - searching out cool shade, no doubt.

"Where's Cottontop?" asked Enid.

"What?" asked Sally, as she stood slowly, stretched her neck and shoulders, and wiggled her fingers.

"He was supposed to be watching over you."

Sally didn't answer.

Enid frowned. "I thought we might have scones for afternoon tea. Alfred is quite partial to them. Could you get some from the freezer, so they can defrost? I'll do a perimeter check."

Sally grunted and shuffled towards the cottage.

"Sally, are you all right?"

Sally halted and shook her head. "I just need time. To adjust." She started toward the cottage again.

Enid cleared her throat. "Are you *sure* you're all right, dear?"

"Why would I not be?"

"The scones are in the chest freezer." Enid pointed to the laundry.

Sally turned and shuffled toward the laundry.

Perhaps she'd got too much sun? Enid glanced at Sally's bare arms. There was no sign of sunburn. Heatstroke? Enid shook her head. Plenty of water and a cool shower. That's what the girl needed. And a sun hat.

Gravel crunched in the driveway. A car braked. The front gate clanked shut.

"That must be Alfred." Enid leaned over the sun lounge to look down the side driveway.

Alfred's car rolled down the driveway and parked behind Sally's car, near the laundry. He got out, adjusted his hat and rummaged in the boot. He had foregone his sleuthing jacket. His long-sleeve dress shirt was folded neatly to the elbows. He still wore a buttoned up vest. In this heat! Enid smiled.

"I wonder where he's been?" Enid asked Sally.

Sally did not reply. Enid turned to face her niece. She was nowhere to be seen.

"Good morning, Alfred," said Enid.

Alfred waved.

"Where have you been?"

"I went for supplies." Alfred slammed the boot shut and waved. He fidgeted with the car keys; they slipped and jangled onto the ground. "Didn't Sally tell you?"

He glanced over his shoulder into the front yard as Enid joined him by the car.

"No. She's a bit tetchy at the moment," replied Enid. "I think she's still angry with me."

"I can see her point." Alfred retrieved his keys and pressed the key fob. The car lights flashed. "*I* got a choice."

"Not you *too*, Alfred." Enid's heart pounded. She didn't need reminding.

"Oh, Enid, I didn't mean..." Alfred sputtered.

"I know, Alfred. I'm a bit tetchy as well. It took all morning to settle Agnes." She patted him on the shoulder. "Do you want to join me on a perimeter check?"

Alfred grinned as they crunched up the driveway.

"Oh, I have something I need to ask you," said Enid.

Alfred paused mid-step.

"About what?" He glanced back into the front yard and hesitated. His smile faded.

"I had a note." She rummaged in her pockets and pulled out a crumpled scrap of paper. "Ah, yes! Did you see Simon's ute near the road when you arrived yesterday?"

"No." Alfred slipped his car keys into his pocket.

"Or when you went out this morning?"

Alfred shook his head. "I'd best get lunch started. Feed the troops and all that." He tipped his hat and hurried inside the cottage.

Enid scratched her head. First there was Agnes' commotion this morning, then Sally's gruffness. Now it seemed Alfred was rushing off to avoid her. What was wrong with everyone today? She walked up to the picket fence and examined the gate. Secure. She surveyed the line of palings. All accounted for. She scanned the front yard. Red-tipped caps peeped out of the uncut grass; the gnomes had returned to their guard posts after rallying to Agnes' aid earlier.

A pale garden gnome with snow-white hair positioned himself next to the gate, at her feet.

"Thank you, Snow," she said. "You don't happen to know where Red is, do you?"

The gnome stared blankly back at her.

"He's got to be somewhere." Enid thrust her hands on her hips. "I don't suppose you've seen Mr B either?"

The gnome remained silent.

"No, I didn't think so." Enid examined the yard again. He had scarpered when Agnes started screaming. "He's probably hiding under Sally's bed, or sulking somewhere."

Enid searched down the side of the cottage and under Sally's car. She checked along the front porch and circled around the side of the house to check on the old couch under the kitchen window. It was a favourite spot of his, especially when the sun warmed the cushions. But he was nowhere to be found.

Enid sighed and plopped onto the couch. It had been a long morning. Perhaps she could just... close her eyes... for just a second?

A drawer slammed shut in the kitchen. Cutlery rattled.

Enid jumped up and peered through the window. Sally wrenched open another drawer and rummaged through its contents. She pulled out the family recipe book, flipped through its pages and grinned. She stared at one of the pages for a moment, then flipped to another. She pursed her lips and flipped through the remaining pages, then slammed the book shut, shoved it back into the drawer and stormed out of the room.

The Marple Brigade was falling apart. And it was Enid's fault! Her shoulders slumped. She couldn't face the Collector by herself - let alone The Dark. They just had to hold up long enough to complete their mission.

Enid buried her head in her hands. "Oh, Mr B, where are you when I need you?"

The screen door creaked open. Alfred stepped onto the porch. He tapped his fingers on the doorframe.

Enid lifted her head. "Yes, Alfred?" she asked wearily.

"It's Agnes," he said. "She's locked herself in her bedroom with '*The Book*' and won't let anyone in."

"Oh, dear." Enid wrung her hands. Mr B would have to wait. Duty first.

It was always duty first.

"I'm coming," she said.

Enid lifted the cotton sheet off the floor and tucked it back over the standing mirror. She glanced at the open bedroom window.

"I don't remember leaving that open." Her heart dropped a beat.

She licked her finger and held it up to the window. There was still no breeze. The air had been still all morning. She held her breath, ran her finger along the fly screen and examined the tip. It was clean. No soot.

Enid gazed out the window and examined the sky. It was clear; there was no sign of an oncoming storm. She ventured a breath and surveyed the back yard. It was empty, save the hawthorn hedge, the beehive and a few watchful garden gnomes along the fence. Something glinted under the sun lounge. Enid huffed. Sally had forgotten to clear up the glass. The girl was distracted. That wasn't useful when it came to a fight. Enid peered into the shadow under the sun lounge. There was something else; something yellow and red. Enid scoffed. She was just as skittish as the others. She pulled down the sash window and twisted the lock in place.

She eyed the cover sheet, grabbed its corners and tied them in a knot behind the mirror.

"That should do it." Her shoulders relaxed. One could never be *too* careful.

Enid walked down the hall and paused outside Sally's room. The door was shut. She tapped on it. There was no answer. Enid took a step, and hesitated. What if Sally's mirror had been uncovered as well?

"One can never be too careful," she whispered under her breath. She pressed her ear against the door and knocked again

Still no answer.

Enid wrapped her fingers around the doorknob. An uneasiness tugged at her brain and vexed her. She took a deep breath and twisted the door handle.

Sally's bedroom was hot and stuffy. The curtains were drawn, holding in the midday heat. A sliver of sunlight peeked through the narrow slit between them. The window appeared to be shut.

Enid's eyes took a few seconds to adjust to the low light level. She peered in the direction of the standing mirror. Reflected light glinted at her. Enid clenched her fingers. The sheet lay, wrinkled in a pile, around the base of the mirror.

She rushed forward, snatched up the sheet and flung it over the mirror. She tied the corners behind it - in two knots, just to make sure it would not slip off again.

One sheet was an accident, but two sheets...? Her heart raced as she scanned the room. She frowned. There seemed to be nothing untoward. She chided herself for not doing a reconnaissance before entering the room. She was getting lax. She glanced at the ceiling to be thorough.

All clear.

Enid rested against the mirror frame and tried to slow her heartbeats. It was nerves, that's all. They were *all* were on edge. There had been a strong gully wind earlier that morning. Perhaps the sheet had fallen, and Sally had closed the window and forgot to replace it? Still, best to check Agnes' room. Enid didn't believe in coincidences.

"Agnes?" Enid knocked on her door. "Please let me in."

There was a scuffle and a muffled reply: "Go away, I'm reading."

"Agnes, please?"

There was no reply.

Enid sighed. Agnes always did her own thing; At least she was sounding more like her usual stubborn self.

"Very well," said Enid. "But please shut your window, and make sure your mirror is covered."

Enid waited. There was no reply.

"Did you open the window in my room?" asked Enid as she entered the lounge room.

Sally sat on the lounge chair reading a book. A ramshackle pile of books sat precariously on the coffee table in front of her.

"No, why?" Sally snapped the book shut and placed it beside her on the lounge chair.

"The sheets had slipped off the mirrors." Enid sat in her favourite armchair opposite the lounge chair and glanced at the book next to her niece. It was a treatise on herbs and their uses.

"Oh," said Sally. "That must've been Agnes. She's been doing odd things all day. You remember the sugar bowl in the ice box, don't you?"

Enid nodded.

"And she tried to put the cat into the washing machine, remember?"

"Oh, that's right." Enid snapped to attention. "Have you seen Mr B? He's been AWOL all morning."

"Not in the house," replied Sally.

"He's never been gone this long." Enid twisted the signet ring on her finger. "He never misses our morning chat."

She stared out the window, hoping to catch a glimpse of his tail twitching in the grass as he stalked a magpie or teased one of the garden gnomes. Alas, there was nothing. Her heart sank. She hoped he hadn't done anything reckless.

"Enough of that." Enid slapped her thighs. "I think we all need a cuppa."

There was a knock on the door.

"I'll get it." Alfred's voice drifted in from the kitchen.

Enid leaned toward the lounge room door to listen; she heard Alfred's voice, in the hallway..

"Tom, what are you doing here again?" he asked.

"I might ask you the same, Dad." Tom cleared his throat. "I've got some news for Miss Turner."

Sally grabbed the herbal treatise and shoved it into the nearest bookshelf behind her. She gathered up the books from the pile on the coffee table and inserted them into any empty crevice she could find and ducked out of the room. Enid raised an eyebrow.

"Which one?" Alfred voice was closer.

"The elder. I need to speak to Miss Enid Turner."

"They're both in the lounge room," said Alfred.

Tom nodded a quick greeting as he entered the room. He wore the same suit, but a different tie, a garish one that Enid surmised he had chosen himself. Alfred followed him into the room and wiped his hands on the apron he'd borrowed from Enid.

"Good afternoon, Detective Knowles." Enid rose from her chair and clapped her hands together. "To what do I owe the pleasure?"

Tom hesitated. "I've just got a few questions, Miss Turner."

"Call me Enid," she said. "Please, sit down." She indicated the lounge chair where Sally had been seated.

"Miss Turner," Tom sat down and opened his notebook, "I understand you reported a missing person on Saturday. A Mr Simon Oldham." He looked up from the notebook. "Your gardener, I believe?"

"Yes."

"And why did you report him as missing?"

"He didn't turn up to look at my hydrangeas on Saturday morning," replied Enid.

"And had he ever not turned up before?" asked Tom.

"I don't know. It was the first time I'd engaged him to work on the garden."

"Then why report him missing..." He consulted his notebook. "Only three hours after his scheduled appointment?"

"He was the grandson of my friend, Olive Oldham, whose murder you are currently investigating." Enid paused. She couldn't tell him the truth; that she needed to track down a soul collector and Simon may be one of its targets. "I thought you'd like to know as soon as possible," she said.

"I see." Tom scribbled in his notebook. "And has Mr Oldham contacted you since Saturday?"

Enid shook her head. *Obviously not.*

"Or your friends?"

Enid and Alfred shook their heads.

"Do you know if your friend, Agnes Farrow, has had any contact with Mr Oldham during that time?"

"I can't see how she could." Enid thrummed her fingers on the arm of her chair. They were wasting time.

"We tried to speak with Miss Farrow at the hospital, but she left yesterday before we could get her statement," said Tom. "I understand she is staying here with you."

"Yes."

Alfred hovered closer to Enid's armchair. "You're sounding all official, Tom."

"May I speak with Miss Farrow?" asked Tom.

Enid gripped the upholstery. In Agnes' current state, she could spill all their secrets - about the Collector, The Dark, magic. All of it. Agnes would *never* forgive Enid if she let that happen.

"She's resting at the moment. She's still not well. I doubt if she would make any sense at the moment." Enid glanced at Alfred. He knew his son better than anyone. Perhaps he could distract him.

"I see," said Tom. "Miss Turner, are you aware that Simon Oldham was found dead this morning?"

Enid gasped. Her mind raced. Another soul lost? That would make *eleven*. One more than expected. If so, they were running out of time.

Alfred dropped into the armchair next to Enid.

"When did you last speak to Mr Oldham?" asked Tom.

"Um... Thursday afternoon, to confirm his start time on Saturday." She swallowed. "How did he die?" She had to know; was he taken by the Collector?

Tom stopped writing in his notebook and looked up.

"Was he attacked, like Olive?" Enid leaned toward him. "Or Sally and Agnes?" *Was he the eleventh soul?*

"No," replied Tom.

Thank God! Enid leaned back in her chair. Her muscles relaxed slightly.

"How did he die?" she asked.

"I can't give you information on an ongoing investigation."

"Tom, please. These are my friends. You suspect they're being targeted, don't you?" asked Alfred. "Surely, you don't think they are involved in his death?"

"No, but—"

"Then tell us, Tom." Alfred slapped his hands on the arms of his chair. "His grandmother was Enid's best friend."

Tom bit his lip and stared out the window. "You have to promise me you won't start nosing around."

Enid and Alfred looked at each other.

"I mean it, Dad," said Tom. "None of your amateur sleuthing."

"I promise, I won't leave the property," said Enid.

Tom narrowed his eyelids. "And you, Dad?"

"What Enid said," replied Alfred. "She's the boss."

"Yes, I can see that." Tom glanced at Alfred's floral apron.

Alfred huffed, untied the apron and draped it over the arm of his chair.

"Okay," said Tom. "The body appears to be severely dehydrated, so the best estimate is he's been dead for several days."

Enid's internal organs plummeted into her stomach. She felt ill.

"It didn't appear to be related to the other attacks," Tom continued. "But you reported him missing, and he was the grandson of the deceased victim."

His words sounded muddled. Enid dug her nails into her palms, trying not to react. Alfred placed a gentle hand on hers.

"That can't be right," she whispered. Her hand trembled. Alfred clasped it tighter.

Tom continued to speak. Enid didn't listen. She'd heard enough. She refused to accept the implication of what he was saying.

"So, you see, we're unsure how he could have contacted you when it appears he was already dead," said Tom.

"Are you implying that Enid is lying, Tom?" asked Alfred in a stern voice, as if telling off a disrespectful teenager.

"No, Dad." Tom voice remained calm. "We're just trying to get an accurate time line of events." He closed his notebook. "I think your friends could be in serious danger. I think you may have stumbled onto something while you were playing detective." He leaned closer to Alfred. "Drugs? Gangs? I don't know. But canvassing the neighbourhood got you noticed, Dad. And I think you're all being targeted because of it."

"It was just a few questions, Tom."

"It could be a serial killer, Dad!"

Enid squeezed Alfred's hand. She'd done this. She'd placed him in danger. How could she ever forgive herself if he was hurt?

"Isn't that right, Enid?" Alfred squeezed her hand back.

"Pardon?" Enid stared at him. She hadn't heard a word he'd said.

"We'll lock the doors and be very careful," Alfred spoke slowly and nodded at her. "And we will help Tom however we can, won't we?"

Enid nodded along with him, mirroring his movements involuntarily.

"We'll make sure Agnes comes down to make a statement when she's feeling better. On...?" He squeezed her hand again.

Enid looked at Alfred. He squeezed it a third time. He wanted an answer, but Enid had more important things on her mind than statements. Like finding the Collector's host, preventing the collection of the last two souls and saving the world before...

"After Wednesday," she said.

"Wednesday?" asked Alfred.

Tom opened his notebook. "Thursday afternoon?"

"Yes," replied Enid. After the full moon. "Everything should be settled by then."

"Then I'll have someone call you to confirm a time." He flipped his notebook shut. "I'll send a patrol car up to check on you tomorrow."

"No need," said Enid.

"I don't think that's a good idea. Three women, up here all alone, two of whom have already been attacked."

Alfred frowned.

"How could he know where we live, Detective Knowles?" said Enid. "And your officers have more important things to do than babysit us."

"I must insist," said Tom.

"And so do I," said Enid.

Alfred cleared his throat. "I'll stay."

"You're not helping, Dad."

"Then it's all settled." Enid stood up and proffered her hand. "Good day, Detective Knowles."

Tom sighed. "Very well, Miss Turner." He rose from his chair and slipped his notebook in his coat pocket.

Alfred escorted him to the lounge room door.

"Promise you'll contact me if you see anything strange." Tom pressed a mobile phone into Alfred's hand. "I'll see myself out."

Alfred slipped the phone into his trouser pocket.

"He's not happy," said Alfred.

"He's worried," said Enid.

Quick footsteps padded up the hall.

Enid's heart skipped. "Mr B? You've come back!"

"Has the cop gone?" Agnes appeared in the doorway and leaned against the jamb.

"Agnes, you're back with us?" Enid smiled.

"He's wrong about Simon," whispered Agnes. "I saw him on Friday."

"What?" Enid picked up the apron and joined Alfred and Agnes in the hall.

"You always have to be *first*, Enid. I wanted to get the information before you for once. I wanted to get first crack at him." She rubbed her head. "Well, he got me instead."

"But Tom said he'd been dead for almost a week." Alfred shook his head. "I don't understand. How could he have attacked Agnes?"

Enid frowned. She didn't like the answer.

"Simon was the host all along." Enid's voice wavered. "It's the only explanation. It's been using his body the entire time, collecting souls." A hot flush crawled down her spine. Her body shuddered.

Alfred placed his hand on her arm.

"Don't you see? It only needs *two* more souls. Not three." She removed his hand from her arm and strode into the kitchen. They were in greater peril than she'd thought.

Plastic beads clinked and bells danced and jangled wildly as Enid pushed aside the bead curtain in the kitchen doorway and strode into the middle of the room. Alfred followed.

"Can you turn on the kettle, please, Alfred."

Alfred flicked the kettle's switch.

"I need to talk to you."

Alfred clenched his jaw.

Enid slid into one of the kitchen chairs and rested her elbows on the table. "I can't do this, Alfred. I can't defeat The Dark alone."

"You're not alone," he said softly.

"We're supposed to be Protectors." She scoffed. "Agnes has barely recovered enough strength to stand. Sally is constantly distracted and, if I hadn't discovered the uncovered mirrors in time..." She clasped her head in her hands.

"Mirrors?" He fumbled with the teacups.

"Someone uncovered the bedroom mirrors. It would've provided a bridge from the Otherworld to negate the Wards."

"Perhaps it's a coincidence?" said Alfred.

"One was a coincidence. But two?" She lifted her head. "Both Sally's and mine? I don't believe in coincidences, Alfred." She grabbed his arm. "Somehow, the Collector has crossed the Wards and, if one of us has been compromised, then there's only one soul left to collect. The Dark could be coming for the rest of us sooner than expected."

The colour drained from Alfred's face.

The bead bells tinkled as Agnes shuffled into the kitchen. "I'm starved," she said as she sat next to Enid.

Enid frowned. Agnes looked exhausted.

"How about a cup of tea and scones?" asked Enid. "They should be defrosted by now." She scanned the bench. There was no sign of the scones.

"I forgot to get them," said Sally.

Enid jumped, knocking her hand against the edge of the table and cursed under her breath. Sally sat at the table opposite them.

"I didn't hear you come in, dear," said Enid.

"I can get them." Alfred edged toward the door.

"No." Enid rubbed her hand as she rose from her chair. "I'll make toast instead. You fetch the honey and lemon butter." She slipped some bread into the toaster and returned to her chair.

Alfred nodded, dashed back into the pantry and returned with two jars. His hands shook as he placed them on the table. Enid raised an eyebrow. Agnes glanced at Alfred, then back at Enid.

"Are you all right, Alfred?" asked Sally.

"Of course. Why wouldn't I be?" He moved towards the bench and opened the cutlery drawer.

Sally leaned toward Enid and whispered: "He was the only one of us outside the Wards today."

"Is that so?" Agnes rubbed her chin.

Alfred had been acting peculiar all afternoon. Enid watched him fumble with the silverware. He winced, snatched his hand out of the drawer and sucked his finger. Enid frowned. He couldn't be a host, could he?

The toaster popped. Alfred stacked the toast on a plate, placed it in front of Enid, and sat at the far end of the table.

"Why *did* you go down the hill this morning?" Enid asked Alfred as she slathered lemon butter on her toast. She slid the honey pot in front of him. "Try some blue box honey, Alfred."

Alfred cleared his throat and dribbled honey on his toast. "I asked a friend if I could borrow his trebuchet, for your lemon butter grenades."

"What a good idea," said Agnes.

"I just hope I can return it in one piece." He took a bite of his toast.

Enid raised an eyebrow. "You have interesting friends, Alfred."

"Ah, yes. He makes them for the Medieval Fair."

"Did you uncover the mirrors, Alfred?" asked Agnes.

Alfred sat motionless, his toast half way to his mouth. Enid held her breath. She couldn't bear to think he was lost to them.

Agnes sipped her tea. Sally nibbled the corner of her dry toast and eyed him.

"No," he said finally.

Enid took a ragged breath.

"You were the only one to leave the property," said Agnes.

"It's not me. If I was working for that Collector thing, how could I cross the Wards?" He turned to Enid. "Look into my eyes, Enid. Please say you know it's not me."

Enid stared into his pale blue eyes. The pupils had almost consumed the iris. A tear hugged the eyelid. She wanted to believe him. But she could never trust her judgement when faced with such heartbroken eyes.

Alfred blinked. The tear receded. His shoulders drooped. His voice was strangely calm when he spoke. "How can I prove it's not me?"

Enid watched the honey drip off the corner of his toast and run down his fingers. She smiled as he placed the toast on his plate.

"You just did," she said.

"You believe me?" His spark returned.

Enid dabbed her finger in a drop of honey on the table and licked it. "Honey is acidic. If you were a host, you'd be retching by now."

Alfred sighed and licked his fingers.

"Then it was a coincidence," Agnes glanced around the table.

"People often imagine things when under pressure," said Sally.

"Quite." Enid glanced over the remains of their afternoon tea. Toast crumbs, smeared with lemon butter were all that remained on Agnes' plate. She eyed Sally's untouched cup of tea and the piece of plain toast on her plate.

Sally had been quick to implicate Agnes' muddle-headedness for the uncovered mirrors. Could Sally have uncovered them? Enid frowned. No, she'd been outside all day - and she'd been alone. She could easily have snuck back into the cottage. What had her niece been doing all morning? Why was she so distracted, and why hadn't she cleaned up the broken glass, as she said she would?

Enid took a bite of her toast and licked the lemon butter from her lips. And what was it she had spied under the sun lounge? She needed to find out.

"You're very quiet, Enid," whispered Alfred.

Enid sucked in a quick breath. "I've left the wet clothes in the washing machine." Better to have the world think she's senile than to have no world at all.

"You're worried about the washing?" asked Agnes. "With the potential end of the world imminent?"

"You can't save the world in dirty clothes," replied Enid.

Sally smiled.

Agnes huffed.

"I'll be in my room." Agnes rose to her feet and strode out of the kitchen.

Enid grabbed her walking stick from the front hall, shut the back door behind her and trotted along the path toward the sun lounge. Sunlight glinted in the grass near the drink table - a hint of blue and silver. She bent down and wrapped her fingers around the object. It was cold, but warmed in her palm.

She opened her hand. A sapphire gleamed at her from the centre of the silver medallion. Its chain drizzled through her fingers. She gasped. It was Sally's amulet.

Enid peered under the sun lounge, unable to spot any sign of the red and yellow she'd seen from her bedroom window. She swallowed, dreading what she may discover hidden there. She stretched her arm under the chair as far as she could reach and searched the ground blindly with her fingers. Something sharp pricked a fingertip.

Her heart raced. She patted the ground, felt several irregular-shaped fragments, and gently scooped them up in her hand. She sank onto the edge of the lounge. She took a deep breath. Her hand shook as she opened one finger at a time.

First she saw a chunk of yellow, then red, then more yellow - all pieces of broken ceramic. Her heart sank as she turned them over in her hand to reveal a red-painted cheek and smudged eye peeking out from under curly white hair.

"Cottontop." Enid's shoulders slumped. He had been sent to watch over Sally while she rested, as Red was nowhere to be found. She scanned the yard for any other fallen gnomes. Thankfully, poor Cottontop seemed to be the only casualty.

"Please, not Sally."

Enid felt ill. She didn't want to accept the possible implications of her discovery. Sally had either removed her amulet, or it had been removed for her. Either way, she had been left unprotected. Enid closed her eyes and took a deep breath. It was highly likely Sally had been infiltrated and was now a host - and she had uncovered the mirror bridges to the Otherworld.

Enid glanced toward her bedroom window. The afternoon sun winked back, as if mocking her.

"Not again!" She jumped to her feet and shoved the amulet in her skirt pocket. Her heart pounded as she dashed to the window and peered inside.

Glare from reflected sunlight dazzled her. She thrust up her arm to shield her eyes and squinted to see clearly. The mirror was uncovered. Again!

Three was definitely *not* a coincidence. Enid's legs quivered as she snatched up the washing basket from the chair under the veranda. They trembled as she rushed inside the hall and called out to Alfred.

"Alfred, will you help me? There's more than I thought. I haven't got the strength to carry it all."

Alfred met her in the hall.

Enid snatched his jacket off the coat rack, grabbed his arm and dragged him into her bedroom.

Enid marched over to the standing mirror in her bedroom. She snatched up the crumpled sheet and draped it back over the mirror's frame.

"What's going on?" asked Alfred.

"Shhh," hissed Enid, as she exited her room.

She locked her bedroom door and ushered him back to Agnes' room. The door was shut.

"Do you smell smoke?" whispered Alfred.

Enid lifted her hand to knock as Agnes opened the door. A look of panic gripped her face. She shoved a handful of partially burnt pages in front of Enid. Their edges were scorched and stained with oily soot. Enid's nose twitched as the stench of burned paper and urea filled her nostrils.

"It's been in my room."

"Quiet," whispered Enid.

She pushed them inside the room and closed the door. The washing basket clattered on the wooden floorboards.

"And it's taken some of the pages of Olive's *Book*." Agnes sat on the bed and took a deep breath. "The ones detailing our magic and—"

"Quiet, Agnes." Enid turned back to the door and whispered under her breath. "*Celare*."

She listened at the door. Nothing. She checked the keyhole. The magic glittered and rippled across the keyhole, obscuring any view through the orifice. The Wards were intact. She crossed to the window and placed her hand on the glass. It hummed under her palm. The room was safe.

"More Wards?" asked Alfred.

Enid nodded. "She can't hear us in here now."

"Who?" asked Alfred.

"The Collector," replied Enid. "It's Sally. It has to be."

"But how?" asked Agnes. "The Wards were—"

Alfred stepped forward.

"When I went out on my errand..." He took a deep breath. "When I went out this morning," he said slowly, "I left the gate open." He winced. "I should have told you."

"That explains it," whispered Enid under her breath.

"Explains what?" asked Alfred.

"Why you've been avoiding me all day," replied Enid. "And how the Collector got past the Wards."

Alfred slumped onto the edge of the bed.

"It's all my fault," he said quickly, "Now one of us could be the new host. Agnes said it was coming." He stared at the ground, avoiding her gaze.

"This is what happens when civilians get involved. I told you it wasn't a good—" said Agnes.

"Mistakes happen." Enid glared at her. "Look what happened to Olive, and she'd been doing this all her life. You've been doing this for less than a week, Alfred."

"No, Agnes is right. I've failed you, and I've failed Sally."

"Yes, and—" Agnes clutched the remaining pages of *The Book*.

"Agnes is not herself right now," said Enid. "Are you Agnes?"

Agnes didn't answer. Enid nudged her in the ribs. Agnes crossed her arms and pouted.

"But the gate is closed now," said Alfred. "How can she still be here, within the Wards? Shouldn't the Collector burst into flames or something?"

Agnes waved the partially burnt page remnants at them.

"That's what I'm trying to tell you," she said. "There were pages about the host. Olive suspected it could camouflage the Collector's true nature, not only from our eyes, but from the Wards as well."

"How could it do that?" asked Alfred.

"The Wards are made to recognise those close to us," replied Enid.

Agnes nodded. "Olive thought that, if the host was someone near and dear to us, their skin could cloak the Collector. The host would hide its scent so the Wards wouldn't be able to sniff it out." She regarded Alfred through slitted eyelids. "That's why I suspected you. You'd been the only one beyond the Wards but, when you admitted to leaving the gate open—"

Alfred winced. "I'm sorry."

"He's apologised about that, Agnes," said Enid.

"Oh, Olive, why didn't you tell us," whispered Enid under her breath.

"You knew her better than me," said Agnes. "Olive was always the General; she only ever told her troops what we needed to know. And she wasn't sure." Agnes presented Enid with the pages. "There's a lot in there she didn't mention to us." Agnes sighed. "And it was her downfall."

"I'm so sorry," whispered Alfred.

"Stop wallowing, soldier," hissed Enid.

Alfred sat upright on the bed.

"It could have been any of you. I even suspected you, Agnes, after you were attacked. And you, Alfred. You've been acting suspiciously all day."

"Then how do you know it's Sally?" asked Alfred.

"Did you see her toast?" asked Enid.

"Toast?" Alfred scratched his head.

"Sally always has lashings of lemon butter," replied Enid, "but today - today, she couldn't even look at it."

"Oh," said Alfred.

"You ate toast and honey. Agnes had the lemon butter and Sally... Sally hardly touched anything. She only nibbled a bit of plain toast."

"But perhaps she wasn't very hungry?"

"Then there's my books," replied Enid. "When your Tom arrived, she just shoved them anywhere in the shelf; she's always insists they should be in alphabetical order. She's fastidious about it. Other than Agnes, she was the only one who had the opportunity to uncover the mirrors."

Agnes shook her head slowly.

"Then there's this." Enid opened her hand and scattered the ceramic remnants of poor Cottontop over Agnes' bed cover.

"Not Cottontop?" Agnes' eyelids fluttered. "Are you sure it was Sally?"

Enid nodded. "He was under the sun lounge, with this." She reached into her pocket, pulled out Sally's amulet and held it up. Light flickered off the sapphire as the amulet spun slowly on its chain.

"Oh, dear," said Agnes. She put out a hand to steady herself.

"'Oh, dear' is right," said Enid.

Alfred put his arm around Enid. "So, we just have to separate the Collector from her."

"And did you read how to do that in *The Book* as well?" Agnes scoffed and shook her head.

"No. I assume you would know how to do that. You are Protectors, after all. You can use magic."

Enid shook her head.

"It hasn't been done before?"

Agnes shook her head.

"Never?" Wrinkles deepened in Alfred's forehead.

"Once a Collector has taken over a host, any attempt to separate the Collector unwillingly, will kill the host." Enid's breathing was ragged. She slumped on to the edge of the bed, next to Agnes. "We can't let it consume her soul."

"You're right." Agnes' words had begun to slur. "She's a Protector. If the Collector delivers her to its master, it can break through the shell." Her eyelids drooped. "Then it only needs one more soul before it can unleash its army."

Enid moaned in agony, as if she'd been kicked in the gut. Agnes snapped her mouth shut.

"You said it needs thirteen souls to get through." Alfred sat beside her and took her hand. "We've still got time to save her."

She patted his hand. "It can create a crack, a hole, enough to begin the attack."

"Then why didn't it come through when Olive died?"

"It tried, and it failed. That's why he went after Agnes."

"And failed?" asked Alfred.

"Only just." Agnes slumped back onto the pillow.

"I'm sorry, Agnes. We've pushed you too far," whispered Enid.

Sally was lost to her. Agnes was improving, but still too weak. Enid sighed. She was the last Protector. The only one standing between The Dark and this world. She closed her eyes. And the stronger The Dark became, the more she could feel the magic slipping from her grasp.

"I can't do this alone," she whispered under her breath.

"You won't be alone," whispered Alfred. His warm breath caressed her ear. "I can protect you."

"I can't let you. You would be consumed, my dear." Enid smiled weakly and shook her head. "A Protector must be willing to sacrifice everything to protect their charges. I knew that when my mother died, when I lost Owen."

"There must be a way to save your Sally?" he asked.

Enid shook her head. "My first duty is to protect this world." She straightened her shoulders.

"But Enid—"

She stood up and breathed slowly, measuring each breath. She had to accept fate. It was her duty. She approached the door and nestled her ear against its polished wood. There was a faint pulse on the other side. The Collector was trying to break through the Wards.

It had begun.

"What about the scones?" he blurted.

"How can you think about your stomach at a time like this?" asked Agnes weakly.

"Sally didn't fetch the scones," he replied, "She didn't go near the freezer."

"What have scones got to do with it?" Agnes wrinkled her nose.

"No, listen." Alfred closed his eyes, and spoke: "*The Dark and its Shadow-horde shrink from the cold. They consume the energy produced by heat.*"

Enid raised an eyebrow.

"I read some of *The Book*, remember?" He continued: "Extreme cold is an absence of heat. It must draw the energy back out. So cold should kill it, shouldn't it?"

"Let me think."

Could there be hope? Enid's heart fluttered. She searched her memories, all the words she had scribed over the decades. She glanced across the room. Her gaze fell on the laundry basket lying on its side next to the bed.

The laundry!

The corner of her lip curled. The worry lines faded from Alfred's forehead.

"I know that smirk." He narrowed his eyelids. "You've got a plan, haven't you?"

"The laundry." She tossed Alfred the laundry basket. "And don't forget your jacket."

Enid held out her walking stick and flattened her other hand against the door. Tiny sparks of electricity arced along the stick, up her arm and circled around her chest. It crackled up her neck. Fine strands of hair floated around her face as the static charge built up and crept along the other arm. Her open palm tingled.

"Take my hand, Alfred."

He reached out his hand, hesitated, then took a deep breath and clasped his hand over hers.

Enid felt energy discharge from her hand. Alfred flinched. She watched the hairs dance on his arm. He didn't let go.

"Ready?"

Alfred gripped her hand until his knuckles paled.

"Relax," she whispered. "It's perfectly safe." She closed her eyes and prepared for the rush of energy.

"*Move lavandariae.*"

There was a rush of wind. Her stomach convulsed. And everything went silent.

chapter thirteen

he air sizzled around Enid. Her ears hissed. She blinked, trying to repel the darkness. She waited for her eyes to recover from the shock of the location shift. She just hoped they'd arrived in the laundry as planned. Relocation Magic could be unpredictable.

She concentrated on her surroundings, searching for any hint of the location and any sign Alfred had arrived safely with her. Rough wood scraped her hand and she felt hard wooden boards under her knees. Her other hand was empty, the walking stick presumably having been ripped from her grip with the force of the Relocation - yet another drawback sometimes experienced with Relocation Magic.

The muffled hissing grew louder. Circling.

Enid's head swam. The ground seemed to shift under her feet. A splinter grazed the edge of her palm as she tried to pull herself to her feet and regain her balance. She winced and felt along the wall looking for the light pull. If she was in the laundry, it should be nearby.

Her fingers brushed against something soft and warm.

"Enid, I hope that's you."

The voice was faint. She strained to listen as a wave of nausea swept over her.

"Alfred?" She clutched his hand and smiled in the darkness. "You're here!"

"Where is here?" His voice wavered slightly.

The hissing became a low, gravelly growl. Enid turned toward the muffled sound. The light cord tapped her cheek. A blood-curdling yowl pierced through her mental fog. There was a muffled groan.

Enid yanked on the cord. Light flooded the room. Her head felt as if a swarm of bees were circling inside it. She closed her eyes and slumped to the floor.

"Enid!" Alfred's voice was muted.

The bees continued their whirlwind.

"Enid, wake up."

He'd need to yell louder than that. Enid felt her consciousness sinking. She tried to open her eyes.

Something tickled her nose. Something soft brushed against her skin. It wriggled and pushed against her cheek.

The cat's wet tongue scraped along her chin. He flicked his tail into her ear and was gone.

"Enid, wake—"

The darkness shuddered. The bees faltered. She reached out her hand. She needed her walking stick. She opened her eyes. Enid's focus cleared slowly. Alfred was crouched on his knees in front of her, clutching his chest. He shoved Mr B away.

"Mr B, you're here!"

Alfred buttoned up his jacket and offered her his hand.

"Up you get, and don't think you're getting out of all the hard work that easily." Alfred assisted her to her feet.

Enid's head throbbed.

"Are we in—?"

"The laundry?" He nodded. "That's an impressive trick, by the way."

The bees buzzed just beyond the edge of her consciousness. She leaned against the wall.

"I'll have you know, not everyone can do Relocation Magic."

Alfred smiled and handed Enid her walking stick.

"Thank you." She stepped forward. Her legs wobbled.

He offered her his arm. She took it reluctantly, rested her hand on it and directed him to the other side of the room.

They stood before the freezer. Enid swallowed. Sally had joked it was big enough to hide a body in; ironically it would soon be used to entomb her.

"If your theory is correct, Albert, this will free Sally from The Collector."

Alfred's eyes widened. "You're going to shove your niece in there?"

"Technically, *you're* going to shove her in there," replied Enid.

"Me?"

"I'll lure her in here and you push her in," said Enid.

"And when it leaves, we pull her out, yes?"

Enid nodded.

"How long does it take," Alfred shifted on his feet and eyed the freezer, "before it leaves?"

Enid didn't answer.

"How long, Enid?"

"The Collector only dies when the host dies." Enid's heart raced.

"But, then Sally is...?" Alfred stared at the freezer, a look of horror on his face. "Then you can heal her with your magic, right?"

Enid leaned her hands on the freezer and willed her stomach to stop twisting. She had to concentrate on the Collector, not Sally, or she would lose her nerve.

"We have to be sure *it* doesn't escape and take her soul with it." Enid opened the freezer lid. Frozen scones and cakes were stacked to the brim. "You empty the chest. I'll lure it here."

"How will you do that?"

"I'll think of something." Enid's vision blurred. The room shuddered. Those damned bees! She shook her head.

Mr B rubbed Enid's legs and growled at Alfred.

"You need rest," said Alfred. "I'll go."

"And how will you defend yourself? I won't have you becoming its thirteenth victim. I have my walking stick. I'll be fine." Enid hoped she sounded convincing.

"But..." Alfred frowned.

"I have no choice. It's the only option, Alfred. We just need enough time to destroy the Collector."

"And not kill Sally," said Alfred.

"People survive freezing temperatures all the time, don't they?" This time, even Enid herself wasn't convinced.

"And you can use your healing magic," said Alfred. It sounded more like a question, than a statement.

Enid clutched her walking stick. It hummed in her hand. She'd need all the energy she could muster to fight The Dark. She hoped there was enough magic left for both Sally and The Dark.

Alfred reached into the freezer and pulled out the largest plastic containers. He winced as one of the lids tugged on the top button of his jacket and fell to the floor. His jacket fell open as he stacked the containers next to the freezer.

"Have you got something to cover these?" he asked.

Fresh spots of blood seeped through fine slits torn in his shirt.

Enid sucked in a loud breath and pointed at his chest. "Alfred!"

"I'll live." He glared at the cat and clutched at his shirt as he buttoned his jacket.

Enid eyed Alfred's chest. She had an idea how lure to Sally out of the cottage and away from Agnes.

Enid stood under the veranda and rested against the wall of the cottage. It was only five o'clock in the afternoon but the sky was dark. A shadow had crept across the edge of the sun and marched steadily across its surface.

An eclipse? Surely it would've been mentioned in the news? Enid frowned. This wasn't a natural phenomenon.

Enid scanned the back yard. The bees had flown back to the hive and were silent. The Dark was coming. She had to hurry.

Enid slowly eased the back door open, just a crack. She peered through the opening into the hallway. All the lights were off. She closed her eyes and reached her mind out along the hall. There were faint noises in the direction of Agnes' bedroom. She reached further still, to Agnes' closed door. The Wards were still intact. Something scratched at the wood.

Icy talons crept over Enid's heart and squeezed. Enid's eyes snapped open. She struggled to breathe, managing only a few ragged breaths. She had to protect Agnes.

Enid clutched her walking stick to her chest, gathered her strength and prayed her gambit would pay off. Her muscles tensed as she opened the screen door.

"Sally, come quick! It's Alfred."

There was movement in the darkness. Two red points flared, then fizzled and faded. Enid's heart jumped. There was still hope. Sally was fighting it. The Collector had not beaten her yet.

Sally's voice rumbled down the hall. "What's wrong?"

"I think Alfred's having a heart attack." Enid slammed the screen door shut and glanced up at the sun. The shadow was almost half way across the surface. Time was growing short. She needed to move quickly.

"*Move cito.*" Enid's walking stick hummed in her hand. She felt lighter. She hovered, just above the surface of the ground. The veranda slipped behind her. The trees blurred and the grass streamed under her feet as she skimmed on the air and sped along the path toward the open laundry door.

"Hurry," Enid called out to Sally.

Alfred kicked away the doorstop and let the door swing closed behind Enid.

"You have three seconds," she whispered to Alfred.

She gripped her walking stick and took her position in front of the open freezer. She searched her memory for the correct words, and waited.

Three.

Two.

One.

The door flew open. Enid didn't look. She opened her mouth as if in shock and pointed to the side wall, behind the tarpaulin-covered containers.

"He was moving some boxes from behind the tarpaulin, and he collapsed."

She saw Sally flinch, in the corner of her vision.

"Hurry, Sally!" Enid kept staring at the tarpaulin.

Sally lunged in Enid's direction.

Enid gripped her walking stick. "*Move portae.*"

The air shimmered and the room twisted.

Enid stood by the laundry door. Sally stood alone at the chest freezer, her arms stretched out in front of her. She screeched and clawed at the spot where Enid had just been.

Alfred charged forward, turned his shoulder as he connected with her body, and shoved her into the freezer. She scratched at Alfred's arms as she toppled over the edge, legs flailing. She landed inside the chest, with a crunch.

Enid gripped the doorknob, and raised her walking stick in the other hand.

"*Claudere porta!*"

The freezer lid slammed shut with a thud. The room blurred as Enid slid to the freezer, vaulted up the edge, and sat on the lid. Alfred climbed up beside her.

Sparks popped and fizzled along the length of the walking stick. Enid's shoulders slumped as the energy drained from her muscles and out the tips of her fingers.

"That was impressive." Alfred put his hand on her shoulder.

The freezer vibrated; the lid jiggled beneath them. Enid tapped the end of her walking stick on the lid. After a few minutes silence, there was a furious scrabbling and scraping noise under the lid.

Alfred frowned and shifted on the freezer lid.

"Don't worry," said Enid. "I've sealed the lid. It can't escape."

Alfred smiled weakly. "Remind me never to get on your bad side."

The lid shuddered but remained closed.

A hot wind growled outside. The door swung open and tapped against the laundry wall. Enid looked out the door. The sky had a strange green hue and was still darkening. The eclipse was almost three-quarters across the sun's surface.

"We just need time," she said. But they were running out of time.

They sat for a long time, trying to ignore the scratching. Finally, the knocking became intermittent and weakened until, eventually, there was silence. They looked at each other.

"How long do we have to sit here?" asked Alfred.

Enid shrugged. Sally - the real Sally - would've known how long it took for a body to freeze. But they couldn't ask her now. She placed a trembling hand on the lid. The internal movement had stopped.

Deep furrows formed in Alfred's forehead. He reached into his trouser pocket.

"Tom gave me this." He held up Tom's mobile phone. "He told me to ring if we needed help."

"We can't ask Tom how long it takes to freeze a body!"

"No," agreed Alfred.

He pressed a button. The phone's face lit up.

"It's one of those new-fangled what's-its." He swiped the screen. "We can look it up." Alfred tapped the screen. "How long has she been in there?"

"Twenty minutes?"

He tapped the screen again. "Here's something about the Titanic. This might be useful. Hypothermia was in..." He swiped the screen. "Twenty to thirty minutes." He dropped his hand on his lap and sighed with obvious relief. "And the freezer is zero degrees, so we should be okay."

"No," said Enid.

Alfred looked up from the phone.

"The freezer is set at minus eighteen," said Enid.

"Enid, I think that's long enough." Alfred frowned, slid off the freezer and pressed his ear against the lid.

"I can't hear anything," he said.

Enid climbed down off the freezer and pulled open the lid. Warm air swirled out the chest and blasted her face. The stench of possum urine filled the room, seeping into every crevice and assaulting her nostrils. Her eyes watered.

"Alfred, I think we'd better go back."

Alfred reached into the chest and placed the back of his hand near Sally's mouth.

"She's not breathing." He grabbed Sally's arm, hauled her body up and over his shoulder, then laid it gently on the ground near the base of the chest freezer. He checked Sally's pulse and frowned. "Enid?"

"Alfred, I'm serious." She tugged his jacket and stepped back toward the open door.

"Enid, her heart's stopped." He placed the heel of his hand on her chest, interlocked his fingers and started chest compressions.

An unearthly howl surrounded them.

Alfred recoiled and fell back onto the floor as a dark mist rose from the freezer. It whirled up to the ceiling and rushed at Enid, dragging the smell of oily soot with it.

Enid slammed the door shut with her heel and stood her ground, blocking its escape. The Collector circled the room, its movements slow and sluggish. It turned to face her. She raised her walking stick.

"Enid, she needs your help!" Alfred scrabbled back to Sally's body and resumed CPR.

Enid's body shuddered. It felt like her heart had frozen - just like Sally's. The pain radiated along her limbs. Her best chance of saving Sally's soul was to destroy the Collector before it returned to its master. She had to choose. Save Sally's body or save her soul.

"Enid!"

"Not now, Alfred. I'm busy." Enid's breaths quickened, each one filling her lungs with more vile mist. "I can't let it escape." Enid's gaze darted around the room. Alfred was hunched over Sally's motionless body, a look of panic on his face.

Static crackled along Enid's fingers. She clenched her hand, letting the energy coalesce. The Collector inched closer to the door. Enid thrust her arm forward, opened her hand and faced her palm to the mist. Electricity arced across the room and plunged into the Collector.

The mist shuddered and faded.

Enid braced herself against the door. She needed more power. The cord of the light pull slapped the tip of her walking stick. Her gaze traced the cord upward, followed the exposed electrical cables along the plaster ceiling to the light fixture. She grinned.

The Collector's eyes flared red. It laughed and surged forward.

Enid thrust her stick forward. A rope of energy flared from its tip and spiralled around the Collector. Enid pulled back, tightening it like a noose. The Collector laughed, as the noose slipped through the mist.

"No!" Enid wrapped the cord around the end of her walking stick and pointed it at the Collector, and reached toward the exposed electrical wires with the other.

"*Agite*," she hissed.

The cord's brackets popped and cracked. Plaster dust showered over her arm.

"*Agite Nunc!*"

The cord snapped and whipped through the air as the room went dark. Pale green light flickered through the doorway and across the laundry floor. Enid flicked her wrist. The cord twisted and plunged into the core of the Collector.

It roared as the mist coalesced and shrivelled. The room filled with the stink of stale possum urine.

Orange flames erupted and licked its edges. The Collector crumbled, showering the floor with black soot. A steaming haze rose from the pile of debris on the floor.

Enid lowered her arms. The electrical cables fell limp against the wall. Her walking stick slipped from her hand as she slumped against the doorframe.

"Enid!" Alfred's face was red. "I can't..."

Enid stumbled forward and fell on her knees next to him. She was exhausted. Enid wanted to close her eyes and rest. But there was no time. She reached out her hand. Sally's body was ice cold, her eyes open wide. Tears filled Enid's eyes. Her focus blurred. She placed her hand over Sally's heart. There was no movement. No flicker. It was cold.

"Is she...?" whispered Alfred.

"No," hissed Enid. "I need my walking stick."

Alfred retrieved it and placed it in her hand. It buzzed. There was still some residual energy left from the power surge. Enid planted it on the floor and closed her eyes.

"*Revivere!* Wake up!." Enid felt the energy wave travel down her arm, across her heart and into her hand on Sally's chest. Sally's body shuddered. Enid opened her eyes. Sally's eyes stared back at her, still and cold.

"*Revivere.*" Enid's hand trembled and glowed red.

Again Sally's body spasmed. Enid felt her niece's heart twist under her hand.

"*Revivere.*" Sparks fizzled around Enid's fingertips. Her tears dripped onto Sally's pale and unmoving body. "Oh, Sally. What have I done?"

A thunderous crack shook the walls. The laundry door shuddered.

Enid's heart froze. Alfred jumped to his feet.

"Bloody hell!" He stood in front of Enid and turned to face the door.

"That was from outside," said Enid.

"But that thing is destroyed."

"Its master doesn't know that." Enid gripped Sally's hand. "It's coming for the thirteenth soul." She felt as if her heart had been torn out. She wanted to close her eyes, to lie silent and still. She wanted to keep Sally company, so she wouldn't be alone.

Another lightning bolt found its mark. The door rattled and loose ceiling plaster drizzled down on them.

"We've got to go." Alfred pulled Enid to her feet. "It's not safe here."

Duty. Always bloody duty. The scar on her arm burned. She had no choice, like Sally had no choice. Enid reached into her pocket and slipped her niece's amulet into Sally's cold, cold fingers. Sod duty. She wanted revenge.

chapter fourteen

a bright flash flickered through the laundry. A thunderous crack rattled the window near the ceiling. A pale orange glow filled the room. Ravens cawed and screeched outside. Enid strode to the doorway. Their shadows flickered across the fenceline as they dived repeatedly at the rumbling fissure. There was no time to wallow.

"The Dark is coming," she whispered to Alfred.

"But the Wards?" he asked.

Enid glanced down the side of the house and along the driveway. The gate was open.

"The Wards are broken," she hissed.

"Sally?" asked Alfred.

"The Collector," corrected Enid.

"Enid, I'm sorry." Alfred put his hand on her shoulder.

Enid shrugged. There was no time for sorrow either. Enid scanned the back yard, and avoided Alfred's sympathetic gaze. She didn't need reminding of her mistake.

A green light swirled through the artificial twilight, drawing energy toward a giant fracture in the air, just above the fence line. Shadowy tendrils twisted within its core of glowing orange and red. The Dark had found the chink in the Earth's armour. And it would not be long before it broke through.

Black flames oozed out, licked its edges, snaked around the beehive and whipped at the attacking ravens, sending them reeling. They leapt toward the hawthorn hedge along the back fence. The leaves shrivelled and burst into flame.

Enid gasped and grabbed the doorframe. For almost two hundred years, the hedge had protected the cottage and its occupants.

The closest guard gnomes raised their weapons and advanced. The flames leapt toward them. Their bright coloured tunics faded. The ceramic glowed pale orange and, with a sickening crack, shards of pottery exploded across the yard.

Enid's fingers bit into the wood.

"Get into the house, Alfred," she hissed through clenched teeth.

Alfred hesitated. The smell of burning wood and ozone wafted through the doorway.

"Now, Alfred! The laundry isn't protected."

Enid strode out into the yard. Mr B zigzagged protectively in front of her and yowled as she dashed along the path into the cottage and slammed the screen door behind them.

"Alfred?" She glanced back along the path. Alfred's worried eyes stared back at her from the laundry doorway. She swung the screen door open.

"Come on, Alfred!"

Alfred shook his head, his reply drowned out by another crack of orange light, and he ducked back into the laundry.

The fissure rippled and fractured further across the sky. Its edges pulsated, as if alive. A dark form twisted inside the fissure and pushed against the shell-like barrier. A crack ran across the shell and spread until the entire surface had crazed. A gnarled fist - the size of man - punched through the fissure. Glowing glass-like shards exploded into the air, dissolving before they hit the ground.

The stench of sulphur and stale urine blasted across the yard. Enid gagged. Her eyes stung. Electricity crackled along the fist's black leathery hide, as it unfurled its smouldering talons; each tip glistened with orange flames.

Footsteps pattered along the hall behind Enid. Agnes stood in the doorway next to her, wearing a fluffy turquoise dressing gown, dragging Alfred's trebuchet behind her and brandishing a sharp kitchen knife in one hand. Enid raised an eyebrow.

"Well, you said I needed a focus." Agnes shrugged. "I found it in the hall table drawer. Weird place to keep a knife, if you ask me."

Enid sighed.

"Where's Sally? I thought she would decide to join us."

Enid didn't answer.

Alfred emerged from the laundry and surged toward the fissure, a bucket in one hand and a jar of lemon butter in the other.

"No, Alfred!" Enid raised her walking stick. It fizzled. *Not now!* Her head buzzed. A wave of exhaustion swept over her. She propped herself against the doorframe, not able to take her eyes from Alfred, and waited for it to pass.

The hand grasped in Alfred's direction. He dodged and hurled the jar at the hand. It smashed on its dark hide. Lemon butter oozed and sizzled over the hand. Its fingers curled, like a dead spider.

Alfred grinned and dropped the bucket on the ground beside him. He snatched out more jars and pelted them, in rapid-fire succession, throwing with one hand as the other reached into the bucket for another citrus grenade.

He cheered as each found its mark.

"Well, let's do this." Agnes stepped forward.

"No, Agnes. You're too weak." Enid held out her arm to block the doorway.

"Pot and kettle, dear." Agnes eyed Enid. "You can't do this alone."

Enid shook her head and pushed Agnes back into the safety of the hallway and out of The Dark's line-of-sight.

"It only needs one more soul, Agnes." Enid's voice barely made it up her throat.

"One? I thought..." Agnes swallowed. "Not *Sally*? Enid, I'm so sorry."

"Hush, there's no time for that. I have to help Alfred." Enid took a deep breath, stepped out under the veranda.

Alfred's hand scrabbled around inside the bucket. His grin faded. He fumbled for the bucket's handle and lobbed it at The Dark. It glanced off the hand and clattered on the concrete pavers.

"Alfred," Enid screamed, "get inside!"

He lunged toward the veranda and through the doorway. Enid slammed the screen door closed and spun to face him. She pressed her free hand onto his chest and pushed him back against the wall.

Limp strands of hair fell over his face. Sweat beaded on his forehead.

"What did you think you were doing?" hissed Enid.

"Helping you." His pale blue eyes stared defiantly back at her.

"I didn't ask you to help me."

"You didn't get a choice," he said.

Enid removed her hand and stepped back.

Alfred's gaze didn't waver. He stared directly into her eyes and didn't flinch.

"Stop flirting," said Agnes. "We've got a world to save."

Enid took a deep breath. Burning pinpricks of soot irritated her throat. Her lungs convulsed.

"Stay where you are." She glared at Alfred. "Both of you."

She tightened her grip on her walking stick, pushed open the screen door and strode to the edge of the veranda.

The tips of red caps bobbed between the blades of grass as gnome reinforcements marched from their posts in the front yard.

Enid smiled and made her stand.

"You've lost," said Enid in the most commanding voice she could muster. "Leave this world while you can. Return to your Otherworld and do not return."

"Or what?" The Dark sneered as it slowly unfurled its talons. "Once my Collector has returned, I need only your soul, Protector."

"Your Collector will not be coming to feed you."

"Yet you cower under shelter." A growling laugh bled through the fissure and rumbled over the surrounding hills. "If my Collector is defeated, then your fledgling Protector is now dead and her soul will still be mine. I shall consume it." There was a pause. "Perhaps, I shall devour your little man-friend as well?"

The fissure flared as The Dark's hand lurched forward and grasped in the direction of the veranda.

"Like hell, you will." Alfred's voice was calm. And close.

Enid flinched. "I told you to stay in the house. Agnes, take the civilian inside and lock the door."

"I will not." Agnes raised her knife and pointed it in the direction of The Dark. "I did a head count. We need every soldier we can get."

Enid raised an eyebrow. It seemed Agnes had finally fully accepted her duty as Protector.

"Only two Protectors and dissension in the ranks?" The Dark laughed. "You shall not defeat me." The hand inched further out of the fissure until the entire forearm rippled in the twilight. "Behold, I am Darkness; the one thing *all* life fears."

"It's the twenty-first century," yelled Enid. "People no longer cower at amateur dramatics." She stepped out from under the veranda and strode into the yard, into the midst of her hidden gnome army. Long grass tickled her legs. "You will not cross into my world!"

"You!" The strength of its voice forced Enid back a step. Her skirt fluttered around her calves.

"The little human girl? All grown up?" The fissure flared. "The years have not been kind."

Enid's muscles tensed. It remembered her. She had tried so hard to forget.

"How long has it been?" It inched closer. "Almost two hundred years?"

There was a scuffle under the veranda, followed by muffled voices and a clicking and ratcheting sounds.

"I told you to stay where you are," Enid snapped.

The Dark chuckled. "Tell me. How is your mother?"

A fire rumbled inside Enid's gut. Each generation had their duty. Her mother had died protecting her as a child. Now it was her turn; she would die protecting Alfred and Agnes, if she had to. She had failed Sally; she would not fail them as well.

"You will not cross over." She pointed her walking stick at the returned enemy.

"Who will stop me?" it roared. "The Protector or the human pet?"

"I will stop you," replied Enid.

"Ha! You and whose army?"

Enid thrust the end of her walking stick into the ground.

The thunderous stomp of hundreds of marching feet reverberated through the ground as the gnomes stood to attention, ready for their orders.

"I brought some friends."

The ring of metal rang out across the yard as the gnomes unsheathed and readied their weapons.

"*Pete!* Attack!"

Jars glinted as they arced through the air toward the fissure. They shattered on the sun lounge, the grass and the pavers. Most found their mark. The putrid smell of sizzling hide burst in waves over Enid, as the swirling winds from the fire gained strength.

Agnes squealed in delight with each successful attack. Another jar smashed into the hand. Lemon butter bubbled over its hide. Then silence.

"Agnes?" Enid glanced back toward the veranda.

"We've run out." Agnes scowled and thumped the empty tea trolley and snatched up her knife.

Alfred pulled the trebuchet back under the cover of the veranda.

The Dark laughed and curled up its talons. Sparks crackled around its gnarled fingers. A ball of black flame swelled inside the talon-cage.

Enid raised her walking stick. "*Scutum.*"

A shimmering energy shield spread out from the tip of her walking stick.

The gnome army swarmed forward, their weapons cutting through the air. The Dark's first attack blasted through their ranks, sending ceramic shards skyward. Still the gnomic horde surged forward.

Its second attack was aimed at Enid. It bounced off the energy shield and fizzled in the air. Heat and ash wafted down, sparking as it touched the shield.

Alfred cried out, whipped off his waistcoat and stomped on pinpoints of smouldering ash. Sweat poured from his face. Agnes tried to pull him back under the veranda. He shrugged her off, flung the waistcoat back under the veranda and joined Enid.

She flicked her wrist. The shield expanded to cover both of them. This had been one of her biggest fears - that Alfred would recklessly put himself in danger. Men were the same in each generation. Why did they never learn? Perhaps she should have listened to Agnes' protestations about civilians.

"This thing's like the Collector, yes?" he whispered in her ear. "Cold will hurt it?"

Enid nodded.

Alfred slipped out of her vision.

"Alfred?"

The Dark curled its talons again. She heard footsteps running away across the yard. Too far away. But she dared not take her eyes off the creature.

"Alfred, come back. I can't protect you beyond the shield."

The hand pointed in the direction of the footsteps. A bolt of electricity leapt from a talon and smashed into a paver.

Agnes rushed forward to take his place.

"Is he...?" Enid asked Agnes. She dared not look.

"It missed," replied Agnes. "He's quick, that one." She mumbled under her breath.

The tip of her kitchen knife glinted orange in the corner of Enid's vision. The magic popped and fizzled on its tip. Agnes groaned in pain.

The Dark laughed. "Your pet has abandoned you, the Protector's magic fails her and your army is weak."

Enid dug her walking stick back into the ground, reached out her arm and spread out her fingers. Her fingertips buzzed as she pulled static energy from both the earth and the air around her. The amplified static crept along her arm and up her neck. Her hair tickled her nose and floated away from her face, until it stood on end and the air crackled around her.

"No, Enid." Agnes took a step back. "That's too much."

"*Hasta.*" The word was barely audible.

Sparks whirled around Enid's hand, her arm and across her body. A cylinder of ice formed in the air before her, its tip elongated into a fine point. She drew back her arm and thrust it forward as if throwing a spear. The ice spear sped toward the fissure.

The hand twisted and grabbed the spear as its tip pierced the fissure's horizon. It split along its shaft and sizzled in the hand's grip. Each end fell in a shower of shards and melted before it hit the ground, raining water droplets on the battling gnomes.

"You are weak, Protector." The Dark chuckled.

A bolt of electricity arced from each talon and converged in the direction of their heads.

Enid whirled her walking stick in front of them. The lightning ricocheted past the fissure and buried itself into a stand of gum trees. The sound of cracking wood echoed down the gully and bounced off the surrounding hills. The trees erupted into flames. The smell of ozone and burning eucalyptus crept across the yard.

Enid winced. The Dark hovered between her and the fire. There was no way she could extinguish the flames without leaving her post. The flames licked the branches and climbed toward the overlapping canopy and roared thirty feet into the air.

The Dark waved its hand in Enid's direction. A wave of heat blasted them and continued onto the driveway, where Alfred had gone. The air shimmered with heat. Enid glanced toward the driveway. A blurred shadow approached them through the haze - a distorted human figure with long arms trailing to the ground.

"No," gasped Enid. The Collector had been destroyed. She'd seen it with her own eyes. It *couldn't* have infiltrated a new host. It scraped as it moved. Her stomach wrenched, as if she'd been kicked in the gut. *No, not Alfred.*

Agnes screamed. Her hands shook as she swung the kitchen knife in the air. Enid jumped back instinctively, and waved her walking stick in an arc above her head. The magic shield snapped to the ground to form a protective hemisphere.

Fire-tipped talons snatched the air where she had stood and scraped along the shield.

"*Scutum.*" Energy pulsed from the stick as Enid pushed forward. She felt the boosted energy draining from her body.

Her arm grew heavy. The shield flickered. The Dark pushed back, knocking Enid off balance. Agnes stepped behind her, grabbed her and stopped her fall.

"Agnes, I can't..."

The shield sputtered.

A shadow fell over the entire yard. Only a thin ring of light illuminated the sky.

The dark figure marched closer, metal scraping.

Sally shivered. The air was freezing. A sharp pain enveloped her chest. Her lungs complained. Oxygen. They needed oxygen. She sucked in a breath. There was sharp smell of sulphur. A metallic taste filled her mouth. Hot air seared her trachea. She sputtered and gasped for air.

Her fingers were numb. She tried to wiggle them, but they refused to move. They were cold, like icicles. She tried to move her toes, her legs, to open her eyes. They all refused. Every muscle in her body ached.

She could hear ravens cawing and fussing in the distance. The last thing she remembered was them trying to warn her.

Flickering light played across her closed eyelids. A loud crack shook the walls. The stench of stale urine engulfed her.

Where was she? She pried one eyelid open a crack. It was almost twilight. Had she slept that long? The crescent moon was visible through a small window near the ceiling. She squinted. No, it was the sun, its surface three-quarters in shadow.

Orange light flickered. She strained to turn her head a fraction. A tall man was silhouetted in the laundry doorway by green swirling light. Buttons glinted on a familiar waistcoat.

Alfred? The words would not come. Sally smiled - or thought she did. Her face muscles protested, so she supposed she had.

Alfred's eyes widened. He rushed back to her side and helped her sit up. He took her hands in his, frowned, and rubbed them vigorously.

Warmth spread up her arm. She flexed her fingers slowly.

Sally opened her mouth and tried to speak. She meant to say: What's happened? But her throat was still silent.

Alfred lifted her chin and looked into her eyes. The wrinkles at the corner of his eyes deepened.

"You'll be fine."

He removed his jacket and draped it over her shoulders. The lingering body warmth spread through her shoulders and chest. She took a deep breath.

Thank you. Again the words were silent.

"I know." He jumped to his feet. "I've got to go. Your aunt needs help."

Alfred tugged the tarp off a pile in the corner. Jars rattled and clinked. One smashed onto the floor. Lemon butter oozed over the floorboards. He cursed under his breath as he snatched up jars and piled them into a bucket.

He lifted the bucket, grabbed one of the discarded jars, and hefted it in his hand.

Sally's heart squirmed in her chest. *The Dark was coming.*

She slid her knees to her chest. They were freezing cold. She rubbed them and tried to pull herself to her feet.

"Stay here. You need time to recover." Alfred stood in the laundry doorway. Flickering light silhouetted him again. "I can't let Enid lose you again."

He sprang out of the doorway, yelled and charged into the yard, brandishing a loaded jar of lemon butter and a rattling bucket.

Outside her aunt screamed.

"Aunt Enid!" Sally's vocal chords strained.

Sally planted her hands on the floor and pushed. Her muscles cramped. She pushed harder. Her temples throbbed. She grabbed the handle of the freezer lid and pulled herself to her feet.

Metal clanked and skittered on the floor. Sally glanced down. The Protector-necklace of silver and sapphire lay at her feet. She scooped it up.

A growling laugh rolled through the doorway. Sally stumbled toward the door. Fingers of smoke curled around its edges and rose to the ceiling. She looked up. A blanket of smoke slowly descended toward her.

The pendant warmed and singed her palm. She winced and opened her hand. A red mark blistered on the skin.

"You don't give up, do you?"

Sally concentrated on the gemstone. Her reflection stared back.

"Where's that magic I was promised?" she croaked.

Her hand throbbed. The sapphire glowed, bathing her hand in a blue light. The pain faded. She concentrated on the light, willing it to expand, to take away the rest of her aches. The light flickered and went out.

"Okay, I get the hint." She swallowed. "Light," she whispered.

Nothing happened. Sally huffed. How did her aunt control it? She searched her memory. Latin. She used Latin. Sally groaned. Her Latin was patchy at best, and what little she did remember came from her medical studies. She frowned.

"*Lux*… no, *accende*," she said finally.

The sapphire glinted. A small blue light crept out of the stone and hovered in front of her. Sally laughed. She just had to focus on the sapphire.

She looped the chain around her neck, tucked it under her shirt, and limped through the doorway.

The smell of wood smoke and sulphur clung to her skin. A daemonic hand with gnarled fingers and long sharp talons stretched out from the rip in the sky. Black flames crackled from its talons, and rained down over the yard. Hell had come to Adelaide.

The sun was black, the eclipse at its peak. Only a thin ring of light illuminated the sky. Sweltering wind squalls roared across the back yard, bringing with it the acrid, white smoke from the growing bush fire.

Enid's eyes watered. She peered through the smoke. The gnomes surged forward, weapons slashing and stabbing, and swarmed over The Dark.

Thunder shook the ground. The fissure pulsated and ripped further across the sky. Black flames spewed from its depths. The hand flung away the gnomes.

The energy shield sputtered. Enid frowned.

"*Scutum.*" The energy drained from her body and channelled into the faltering translucent shield. It curved around her and Agnes. The edge stretched down, barely reaching the long grass.

Broken ceramic shards rained onto the metal roof of the veranda, bounced off the shield and fell at their feet.

Enid slumped to her knees. She could feel the remnants of energy draining from her fingers, her muscles, the very cells of her body. She planted her walking stick into the ground and willed the earth to give up more energy.

"No!" Agnes gasped.

Enid felt the syphoned energy flow through her muscles, her heart. It pulsed through her arteries. She scanned the yard. Her gnome army rallied and rushed The Dark. The humanoid figure marched closer, through the smoke haze. They were flanked.

Enid wiped away smoke-filled tears and struggled to focus. She glared in the direction of the trespasser. The Dark wasn't playing by the rules. There should be only one Collector until The Dark itself has crossed, followed by its Shadow-horde.

She growled. She'd already lost her Sally. She would not allow it to take any more of her loved ones. She raised the tip of her walking stick and pointed it in the direction of the oncoming figure.

"No, Enid!" Agnes stayed her hand. "It's Alfred."

A metal cylinder clunked on the ground several feet in front of them, in the direction of the fissure. Alfred hefted a second fire extinguisher in his hands and grinned.

Enid sighed. Alfred was alive.

"Where did you get those?" asked Agnes.

"They were just sitting around in the Bingo Hall. I thought our need was greater."

"Our cavalry has arrived." Agnes smiled.

"No, the archers," he said, "to give the cavalry time to regroup."

Enid's heart plunged into her stomach. She grabbed his sleeve.

"But we are it. There is no one else."

"Then don't disappoint me." He pulled the tag from the cylinder. "The needs of the one, and all that."

Alfred aimed the black nozzle at The Dark and pulled the trigger. The extinguisher hissed. A white jet of icy mist spewed from it. The gnomes scattered and regrouped.

He marched forward until he drew level with the second extinguisher, and squeezed the trigger tighter. The jet expanded into a billowing cloud, which sizzled where it touched the hand's black hide. It flinched.

Enid grinned. Alfred's crazy plan was working.

The extinguisher sputtered.

"Alfred, no." Enid's jaw clenched.

"He's trying to buy time," said Agnes.

"But at what cost?" Her heart raced. She'd grown to like Alfred and his three-piece sleuthing suit, despite her best efforts to resist.

Alfred dropped the sputtering extinguisher and snatched up the backup cylinder. The tag clattered against the metal casing. He clenched the trigger and inched forward, smothering the hand and held his ground as ragged tufts of mist spurted from the nozzle. Alfred yelled triumphantly.

Enid smiled. He made a resourceful soldier.

The extinguisher spluttered and hissed. It was empty. Enid's smile fell.

"Leave." The Dark's voice was low and guttural. The hand flexed its talons and flicked its wrist in Alfred's direction.

A sonic wave burst from the fissure. The air rippled visibly with the force. Its leading edge smacked into Alfred. His body crumpled and flew through the air, riding the wavefront. The extinguisher clattered onto the gravel driveway, skidded and smashed into the laundry wall.

"Alfred!" Enid shrieked. Her heart pounded.

He landed twenty feet away with a sickening thud and squirmed under the force. He gasped for air until his body went limp.

Enid cringed. The Dark roared with laughter.

"What do we do now?" asked Agnes.

Enid stared at Alfred's motionless body, unable to tear her gaze from him. She willed him to move, to stand. She wanted to run to him, make sure he was uninjured. She struggled to catch her breath. She couldn't abandon her post and leave Agnes exposed to the same fate.

"Enid?" Agnes gripped Enid's arm. "What do we do?"

Enid's gaze flicked back to Agnes, and the battle. The gnomes had resumed their attack, distracting the enemy for the moment. She wasn't a General. She hadn't studied tactics, like Olive, but she knew she'd need more than a magic-weary companion and borrowed magic to defeat The Dark. She took a deep breath to clear her mind. What would Olive have done?

Enid's amulet glowed green under her blouse. A cold shiver ran down her chest. *Cold!* Of course. Her mind whirred. Alfred had realised it all along; he had told her and she hadn't listened.

"Cold," she said. "Cold destroyed the Collector. Perhaps it will work against its master as well?" She glanced at the sky. "I don't like summer. I much prefer winter, don't you, Agnes?"

"Change the weather?" gasped Agnes. "We don't have enough magic, not even at full strength. We *can't* do it."

"We are Protectors, Agnes. We don't have a choice," snapped Enid. "Sally is gone. Alfred can't help us. We are the last line of defence."

"If it works, it will drain us both." Agnes swallowed.

"I know." Enid tried to keep a brave face.

"Together, then?" said Agnes.

"Together to the end," replied Enid. She placed Agnes' hand on the walking stick and lowered it into the hole already dug into the ground. It reverberated under her palm.

"*Boreas*."

The stick shuddered. Thick forks of lightning arced up from the ground as the Earth released its power. A silver light radiated from the walking stick.

Enid's skin crawled. She gritted her teeth as pricks of heat punched through the skin and sparks ran down their fingers, lighting up their hands and revealing the outline of the bones.

"I can't..." Agnes' voice was faint, her skin was grey and her face pale.

Agnes yelped as she was thrown clear. Enid's fingers cramped, locking her grip onto the stick. All her muscles spasmed. She tried to turn her head, to check on Agnes, but she was frozen, staring at The Dark as its hand inched further out of the fissure.

A hand landed on Enid's shoulder. Enid's heart lurched.

"It looks like *The Marple Brigade* might need some help."

"Sally, you're alive!"

Sally nodded. A scarlet-clad gnome wriggled under Sally's arm.

"Red!" exclaimed Enid, "Where have you been?"

"In my car," replied Sally. "I couldn't leave him to miss out on all of the fun."

Red glowered at Sally. She bit her lip and placed him on the ground.

He raised his scythe and rushed into the yard.

"How do you say 'united' in Latin?" asked Sally as she helped Agnes to her feet.

"*Conferre*," replied Enid.

"Then '*Conferre*' it is."

Sally placed a hand on Enid's shoulder and took a deep breath. Agnes did the same. A blue glow radiated from under her blouse and enveloped all three of them. Sally nodded.

"*Conferre!*" They spoke in unison. Green and red light pulsed from their amulets and formed a white glow around them.

The swirling fire squall faltered and stilled. An icy wind whipped the trees. The flames flared and collapsed on themselves. A flurry of glowing cinders flew into the air and faded.

Enid shivered. She glanced nervously at Sally. She seemed calm and detached, unaffected by the bitter wind. She stared wild-eyed at the fissure. A pinpoint of blue light glowed in her pupils.

The Dark bellowed in anger. Frost formed on its hide. It crept up its forearm and spread out, forming a translucent layer over the fissure.

A chill wind tapped Enid's back. Her legs wobbled and her arms ached. The walking stick shuddered and twisted in her hand. She held on tight.

The Dark struggled to escape the frozen shell. Its movement slowed. Its talons twitched and froze. Icicles formed on the exposed tips.

Sally and Agnes' hands slipped from her shoulders. Enid stumbled forward. Her heart no longer raced; it squatted in her chest. Her hands throbbed, her fingers itched and her palms burned. The walking cane slipped from her grasp and bounced on the grass.

She retrieved one of the discarded fire extinguisher cylinders and slammed it against the immobile hand. There was a satisfying crack.

"That's for Olive," she hissed. She struck the hand again.

"And for Agnes." A large crack appeared. Enid grinned. She struck it again.

"And for Sally." The talons shattered and fell to the ground. The crack widened and cracked along the length of the forearm.

"This is for all the innocents you consumed." Enid pounded the cylinder against the remaining stub.

Black shards splintered onto the grass. Enid raised the cylinder and brought it crashing down onto the shards, crushing and grinding them into dust. She loosened her grip on the cylinder. It fell to the ground with a resounding thud.

"And that was for Alfred." She staggered back a step and collapsed to the ground.

Sally stepped forward and handed Enid her walking stick. Enid turned it in her hand. Its decorative etchings had smudged and blurred with the heat. The tip was singed.

It buzzed in her hand. Enid smiled.

"You do it," whispered Sally.

Enid pulled herself to her feet, grasped the walking stick and straightened her shoulders.

"*Claudere porta.*" Enid's body tingled. Lightning forked from the tip of the walking stick and reached out over the full length of the fissure.

A muffled roar rumbled on the other side of the thickening ice shell. The fissure convulsed and snapped shut. The back yard fell silent.

"... and with the unseasonal south winds from the Antarctic, and the resulting low pressure band coming across the Bight, the Bureau of Meteorology has warned the temperatures will continue to plummet. Last month was officially the coldest November since 1847. And it looks like we're in for more this month.

Some areas can expect..."

Enid clicked off the radio, placed her journal on her pillow and went in search of a cuppa.

A chill breeze crept along the hallway. She sniffed. The smell of wood smoke still hung in the air. It permeated her clothing, the curtains, everything - even the cat.

She peered through the screen door. A small withered hydrangea seedling stood alone in a bare patch of scorched dirt - a wound to remind her of the borrowed magic that had saved all their lives and defended this world.

Blackened tree trunks lined the back fence. Too close for comfort. Their scarred branches shivered in a cool breeze. Hints of oily soot wafted in the back door. Much too close. She nudged the back door shut and wandered toward the kitchen. The coffee machine gurgled cheerfully. Enid smiled and continued into the lounge room.

She sat in the chair opposite the lounge. The kettle whistled in the kitchen. She kicked off her fluffy slippers and swung her feet up onto the coffee table, next to Mr B. His ears twitched in her direction, then relaxed.

Teacups rattled as Alfred entered and placed the tea tray on the coffee table. Mr B's ear fluttered. He opened one eye and followed Alfred's movements.

"Can't you two try to get along?" Enid rolled her eyes.

Alfred shrugged and sat in the armchair next to her.

"It's honey with the scones again, I'm afraid. We're out of lemon butter." He picked up the singed printout of Olive's *Book*, slipped off his shoes and rested his feet on the footstool. The tip of his toe poked through a hole in his plaid sock.

A patch of sun crept over the arm of Alfred's chair.

"You've taken Mr B's favourite spot," whispered Enid.

Alfred peeked over the top of the pages and eyed the cat. "So, I have."

His shirt cuff rode up his arm as he turned the page, revealing fresh pink scars from the gravel rash he'd sustained when he'd been thrown onto the driveway.

"I wish you'd let me heal those scars, Alfred."

Alfred pushed up his sleeve, examined his arm, and shook his head.

"It's just a few scratches," he said. "You need to rest and conserve your energy. You still haven't recovered from showing off." Alfred rubbed his arm. "Besides, I think it makes me look rakishly handsome, don't you think?"

Enid laughed.

"Drink your coffee before it gets cold," he whispered. "You're getting the next one yourself."

She sipped her coffee. It was sweet.

"Honey?" she asked.

"Of course," he replied. "Not too much, I hope?"

"No, it's perfect."

Mr B huffed and covered his eyes with his paws.

"We're back." Agnes bustled into the lounge room and eyed the teapot. "Oh, tea!"

"Hello, Alfred." Sally shuffled into the room and slumped onto the lounge. "They say all the electrics are fried and I'll need a new car. Is this going to happen every time I use magic?" She picked up a scone and drizzled honey on it.

"I'm sorry to hear the bad news about your car, Sally," said Enid.

"Is that why you don't drive?" Sally asked her.

"You could say that," she replied.

Enid and Agnes looked at each other. Enid sipped her coffee. It was a long story.

"I told her it wouldn't happen as much if she had a classic car, like mine." Agnes felt the side of the teapot. "Less electrics."

"Would you like some tea, Agnes?" Alfred rose from his chair. "I'll get more cups."

Mr B waited until Alfred left, then leapt onto the vacant armchair and curled up on the cushion.

Alfred returned with two of the best china teacups with roses painted around the rims.

"I thought we could make a new batch of lemon butter tomorrow," said Enid. "The pantry is looking a tad empty." Enid scooped up Mr B and put him on her lap.

"Perhaps I can help you?" asked Alfred as he settled back into the armchair.

"I'd like that," replied Enid as she sipped her coffee from her favourite teacup.

THE END

Acknowledgements

Thank you to my beta readers, David, Katie and Sharon.
Thank you to Symon Williamson for information with regards to classic and vintage cars.
And, finally, to my friend, Dr Sara L Uckelman (Durham University) for the Latin translations.

About the Author

Karen Carlisle lives in Adelaide with her family and the ghost of her ancient Devon Rex cat. She loves fantasy fiction, gardening, historical re-creation, and steampunk and can often be found plotting fantastical, piratic or airship adventures.
Karen has always loved chocolate and rarely refuses a cup of tea. She is not keen on South Australian summers.

www.karenjcarlisle.com
https://twitter.com/kjcarlisle
www.goodreads.com/kjcarlisle

Other Works by Karen J Carlisle

The Adventures of Viola Stewart series
Available in paperback:

Doctor Jack & Other Tales
Eye of the Beholder & Other Tales
The Illusioneer & Other Tales

Also available separately as eBooks:

Three Short Stories
Doctor Jack
Three More Short Stories
Eye of the Beholder
From the Depths
Tomorrow, When I Die
The Illusioneer

With a Twist of Nib: For When Time is Short
(A short story collection)

The Aunt Enid Mysteries
Aunt Enid: Protector Extraordinaire

bonus
extras

short story

My short story, *At Aunt Enid's,* was first written in 2013 and published in my 2017 short story collection, *With a Twist of the Nib.* The main character's name was originally Lucy.

But the characters were not content with such a short adventure.

Both the short story and this novel were inspired by childhood memories of watching my great aunt Enid make lemon butter, and the two hydrangeas that sat at the bottom of her front stairs.

The events in this short story are referenced in chapter ten.

lemon butter recipe

I've also added a recipe for lemon butter that my grandmother and great aunt Enid used to make.

at aunt enid s

© 2013 Karen J Carlisle

Sally was not fond of visiting Aunt Enid. Oh, she was nice enough, but she had never really embraced the electronic age. She had no internet access or pay television - only dusty cabinets crammed with ceramic knickknacks. Sally loved her dearly, but holidays at Aunt Enid's were boring.

'Use your imagination,' her aunt would say. 'Reality can be so much more exciting.'

Thank goodness for the local library.

Aunt Enid had a passion for garden gnomes. It was almost pathological. She collected them from everywhere. There were small cute ones, large ugly ones and novelty ones with axes in their heads. They hailed from England, Germany and local garage sales. There was even one from Iceland.

Sally picked her way through the gnome assembly, which stood in formation over the entire front yard. They stared at her. Or was it just her imagination?

"Mind the gnomes, dear!" yelled Aunt Enid.

Every night Aunt Enid went out to Bingo, leaving Sally to entertain herself. Tonight she hugged Sally as she left yet again.

"Are you sure that you won't be bored?" asked Aunt Enid.

Sally pictured herself sitting in the Town Hall, amongst an army of cardigan-clad pensioners, marking off Bingo cards in an effort to win a basket of goodies. She winced.

"I'll find something to do," replied Sally.

Aunt Enid smiled and trekked up the garden path.

There was nothing but reality shows and repeats on the local television station. Sally had read the contents of her aunt's bookshelf on previous visits. It hadn't taken long to organise them into alphabetical order. Again. She wiped the last knickknack with a cleaning cloth and nestled it back into its cabinet.

All done. She folded the cloth, placed it on the coffee table and wandered to the front window and stared at the ranks of gnomes. They stared back. Sally sighed and proceeded to name each and every gnome in the collection.

Storm clouds gathered. The moonlight faded. A wind caught the rose bushes. A branch lashed out and knocked one of Aunt Enid's precious gnomes onto the path.

He looked so sad, lying with one ceramic arm shattered on the concrete.

Aunt Enid will be so upset.

Sally braved the brewing storm to retrieve the pieces. The door rattled behind her as she laid them on the table.

Muffled noises banged in the street. Sally peered out the window. The wind had died down, yet the front picket fence was shaking. The rose bushes were not. Strange shapes writhed at the edges of the street light, just beyond the fence perimeter.

"Ash wood," said Aunt Enid in her ear.

Sally jumped; she hadn't heard her return home.

"It is good for protection, but it won't hold them for long."

Aunt Enid struck her walking cane on the floor. The air reverberated. A wave pulsed outward from the, now glowing, stick.

Sally grabbed the edge of the side table, struggling to keep her balance.

A cracking sound echoed through the front yard. Then another. The picket fence buckled. Dark shapes rolled over it, onto the lawn.

The gnome guards took a step forward, in unison. Those with fishing rods now brandished swords in their place. Others removed the axes from heads and pointed them towards the shadows. In turn, each gnome rushed the intruders, demolishing them from below. As each row of gnomes fell, another took its place. With military precision, they fought on until the dark shapes dissolved into a grey mist.

"Open the door," said Aunt Enid.

Sally unlatched the door, threw it open and clung to the wall beside it, leaving a clear line of sight. Aunt Enid held her cane at arm's length and blew gently along it, towards the doorway. The grey mist stirred then retreated beyond the picket fence.

The surviving gnomes halted and turned toward the house. They marched back to their spot, leaving the broken remains of their comrades behind. When they had all returned to formation, they turned, as one, to face the street.

There was silence.

Aunt Enid slammed the front door shut and locked it. She strolled into the lounge room and fell into her favourite chair.

"Is that exciting enough for you?" she asked.

Sally nodded slowly, trying to let the night's events sink in.

Aunt Enid sighed.

"Then you had better fetch the superglue," she said.

THE END

aunt enids
lemon butter
recipe

Ingredients:

2 eggs
1 cup sugar
Juice of lemon
1 tablespoon butter

Method:

Whip 2 eggs and 1 cup of sugar until light and frothy.
Add lemon juice and butter.
Cook in double saucepan (or in basin standing in saucepan of water)
Stir frequently.
Pour into pre-sterilised jar and let cool

www.ingramcontent.com/pod-product-compliance
Lightning Source LLC
Chambersburg PA
CBHW031239120726
47905CB00002B/657